EXILE'S QUEST

Also by Gail Z. Martin

Ascendant Kingdoms
Ice Forged
Reign of Ash
War of Shadows
Shadow and Flame
Convicts and Exiles

Assassins of Landria
Assassin's Honor
Sellsword's Oath
Fugitive's Vow
Exile's Quest

Chronicles of the Necromancer / Fallen Kings Cycle
The Summoner
The Blood King
Dark Haven
Dark Lady's Chosen
The Sworn
The Dread
The Shadowed Path
The Dark Road

Darkhurst
Scourge
Vengeance
Reckoning (coming soon)

Deadly Curiosities
Deadly Curiosities
Vendetta
Tangled Web
Inheritance
Legacy
Trifles and Folly
Trifles and Folly 2
Trifles and Folly 3 (coming soon)

Night Vigil
Sons of Darkness
C.H.A.R.O.N. (coming soon)

**Other books by Gail Z. Martin
and Larry N. Martin**

Jake Desmet Adventures
Iron & Blood
Spark of Destiny (coming soon)
Storm & Fury

Joe Mack: Shadow Council Archives
Cauldron
Black Sun
Chicagoland

Spells, Salt, & Steel: New Templars
Spells, Salt, & Steel, Season One
Night Moves
Monster Mash
Creature Feature

Wasteland Marshals

EXILE'S QUEST

Assassins of Landria Book 4

BY GAIL Z. MARTIN

Find out more about Gail Z. Martin's books:
Twitter: @GailZMartin
Goodreads: https://www.goodreads.com/GailZMartin
Newsletter: http://eepurl.com/dd5XLj
Blog: www.DisquietingVisions.com
Website: www.GailZMartin.com
Instagram: https://www.instagram.com/jmorganbriceauthor/
Pinterest: http://www.pinterest.com/gzmartin

TABLE OF CONTENTS

CHAPTER ONE

"Your magic has grown stronger," Malachi, the infamous mage of Rune Keep, said as he set a cup of hot tea on the table in front of Rett.

"It wasn't worth the price." The bitterness in Rett's tone wasn't directed at Malachi. The necromancer had given him shelter, healed the worst of his physical wounds, and brought him back from the brink of death, tethering his fragile soul to a broken body and scarred mind.

Rett still hadn't decided whether that was mercy or torment.

Malachi sat across from him and took a sip of tea before answering. "No benefit can be worth the torture you endured. But to come away with something valuable—it's better than nothing."

"I guess. So far, I can't see that the new abilities are much use."

Joel "Ridge" Breckenridge and Garrett "Rett" Kennard were King's Shadows, dispatched to deal with the highest level of threat to the Kingdom of Landria and its monarch. Unlike the other Shadows who worked alone, Ridge and Rett fought as a team, best friends since their orphanage days. Their methods were unorthodox, but their unmatched success rate spoke for itself.

Until now.

When traitors detonated explosives to kill the king, Rett had been next to Kristoph, buried in the rubble with him. Someone dragged Rett from the wreckage, but "rescue" wasn't their intent.

The Duke of Letwick had been one of the planners behind the assassination, under the sway of Yefim Makery, the mystical "Witch Lord." Letwick and a man he called "Doctor" had taken Rett to an abandoned fortress, battered his body, and used magic and powerful hallucinogenic drugs to assault his mind.

Ridge and their valet Henri were missing, presumed dead. They believed the same about Rett, and by the time they learned the truth, Rett had endured months at the hands of "Duke" and Doctor. He'd been barely alive and not quite sane when Ridge mounted a rescue.

He and Ridge had been falsely accused of treason, wrongly blamed for killing the king. Kane, an unpredictable spy, brought them to Rune Keep, a tower intended to imprison the most notorious witch in all of Landria. Malachi had broken its security long ago, maintaining the fiction of being imprisoned because being moved would be inconvenient.

Malachi and Kane had given them protection and shelter, despite the bounty on Ridge's head and Rett's precarious condition. Malachi had used his magic to anchor Rett and keep him from drifting away and pushed his formidable power to his limits to drag Rett back from the edge of madness.

When Rett woke, raving and untethered, Malachi had patched him back together as best he could, and now that the powerful potions left Rett with unknown, untamed magic, it was Malachi who helped him make sense of it.

"You have visions. They come true. So far, they've been jumbled, but as you gain control of your abilities, that may change," Malachi said. "The dream walking—it's a very rare ability. Powerful. An asset, when you learn to direct it."

Rett sighed. "I wish I could see it that way. Do you know what I see?"

Malachi shook his head.

"I see someone who was one of the best two assassins in the kingdom who failed his mission to protect the king. Who broke under torture. Who's so goddamn unreliable that his partner has to chase leads with someone else. Because I'm a liability. I can't do my job, and I can't protect my partner, and now I've got these wild powers that are likely to get someone killed."

Rett broke off his tirade with a strangled sob. "I should have died back at the fortress. Now Ridge is saddled with a useless partner that he's too honorable to leave behind. Half the time, I can't tell what's real and what isn't. I'm afraid to sleep, and I'm scared to wake up."

"It's better than before," Malachi replied. "Even if you don't see the progress, I do. Ridge does. It won't be like this forever. It took time to hurt you—and it takes time to heal."

"That's just it—there isn't time to wait for me. The Witch Lord is still out there. Duke's witch—the bastard who made the potions and salves that tore my mind apart—hasn't been caught. Landria has no king and no heir. The Witch Lord wants to control the throne. I took a vow to protect the kingdom, and I failed." Rett knew the mage could hear the self-loathing in his voice. "I'm in the way."

"Ridge and Henri wouldn't agree."

"They're sentimental."

"You'd do the same for them," Malachi challenged.

"Maybe not."

"Now you're lying."

Rett rolled his eyes. "That would be different."

"Not in any way that mattered."

He and Malachi stared each other down. Rett blinked first. "Yes, it would. But it feels different when I'm the broken one."

Malachi wisely let the argument drop. "Why don't we try some exercises to gauge whether the reach of your ability has changed. Edvard is happy to help."

Edvard was a ghostly ally who liked the adventure of helping in the quest to stop the Witch Lord. He'd been an invaluable asset and proved that spirits made great spies.

Rett nodded, glad to change subjects. "All right. Now what?"

"Concentrate on Edvard, and see if you can hear each other. Edvard will gradually get farther away. Then you can tell me if anything's changed."

Rett shut his eyes and turned his focus inward. He and Ridge had always shared a common, forbidden magic—the ability to see the soul-stain on those sworn to dark witches. Visions were less common, but he'd had several before his capture. Those had grown stronger and more frequent since then.

His ability to see and hear ghosts was much newer and largely untested. He suspected it was a side effect of having his mind ravaged by the drugs Doctor had plied him with. The "flying ointment" that made him hallucinate also unlocked another "gift"—the ability to send his consciousness traveling while his body remained elsewhere.

Just having the Sight was enough of a danger. I never wanted or asked for more, he thought.

Rett saw Edvard standing by the wall. A second later, the ghost hovered outside the tower. *I can still see you,* Rett said silently to Edvard.

"Same here."

Edvard moved farther, checking in every time he changed positions. Finally, the ghost faded from Rett's senses, and he could no longer hear the spirit's voice in his mind.

"Very good," Malachi said, and Rett opened his eyes. The necromancer had been able to see and hear Edvard as well, which saved Rett needing to explain. "I'd say your range has almost doubled. How do you feel?"

Rett hadn't felt good since before Kristoph's death, but he bit back a snappish answer, reminding himself that Malachi was trying to help. "Not terrible. A little more tired, and I think if I tried to keep up a conversation at the edge of my range, I'd have a bad headache."

Malachi nodded. "Understandable. I know it may not seem like progress to you, but gaining that much strength would take a lot longer through normal training. It could prove valuable in a fight when you needed to reach Edvard."

"That's what I'm trying to focus on—how to use these new abilities to protect us." If he couldn't get rid of the dangerous "gifts" and they didn't kill him, Rett figured he might as well learn how to make the best of them.

Edvard winked back into the room, a willing helper for Rett's studies. He suspected that Edvard appreciated that both he and Malachi could see and hear him, and odd as it might seem to an outsider, Rett had grown fond of the ghost.

"We need to figure out how to keep me from 'wandering,'" Rett pointed out. When Doctor's poisoned salve had nearly killed him, Rett's spirit had traveled without his body—to their allies at Harrowmont and then to a mysterious monastery, Green Knoll, that seemed real enough but apparently didn't exist.

"The issue is to give you control of when and where you go and assure you can always return safely," Malachi said. "Magic, once gained, can't truly be renounced. Trying to ignore an ability doesn't turn out well. It pretty much guarantees that the energy will build up and burst out—usually when least convenient."

"Wonderful," Rett muttered. "That alone will put Ridge in an early grave from heart failure, worrying that I'll get stuck somewhere and not be able to come home."

"It's a reasonable fear," Malachi replied. "Which is why you need to learn to manage the ability, to decrease the risk."

Rett didn't think he'd ever change his mind about the danger of separating his soul from his body, but he didn't think saying that aloud would help.

Malachi brought him a plate with cheese, honey, and an apple. "Eat," he said. "It'll keep your headache from getting worse."

Rett was just about to reach for the apple when everything around him blurred as a vision came on, changing the scene abruptly from the room at Rune Keep.

He saw a luxurious parlor in what he guessed was a nobleman's home. A servant brought a tray with tea and cakes to the two well-dressed men who sat in armchairs near the grand fireplace.

He sensed that the servant had mixed feelings about one man—the noble, who looked vaguely familiar. But the valet's loathing and terror of the noble's guest made Rett gasp and his heart stutter.

The scene changed abruptly. Rett glimpsed a country road, a signpost, and then he was inside a grist mill. The miller bent to his task, sweating and covered with flour. When the man turned, Rett knew this was an older version of the valet from the mansion.

Questions swirled about why the miller had gone from a noble house to a farm town. Reality flickered again, time passed, and now Rett saw the miller fighting two masked, dark-clad assailants and heard him cry out in fear and pain. Then as suddenly as the vision had started, the scene disappeared.

Rett heard Malachi and Edvard calling his name as he slid bonelessly from his chair, landing with a thud on the floor before consciousness left him.

CHAPTER TWO

"Not again."

Ridge sat by Rett's cot, watching his best friend seize and jerk. *Another vision. It has to be.*

"Come on. Wake up." Ridge was afraid to do more than put a leather strap between Rett's jaws to keep him from shattering his teeth. Trying to hold him down just made things worse, he knew from past experience. The fit possessed Rett violently enough to give him extraordinary strength, and if he fought against being restrained, he could tear muscles or dislocate joints.

"Please, help him." Ridge turned to Malachi, who stood in the doorway watching with concern.

"He's in no danger of dying," the necromancer replied. "And the 'wound' is to his mind, not his body. I can mix up something to make him sleep more soundly, but that might not be a kindness."

Rett's head snapped from side to side as he muttered. Duke Letwick's torturer had drugged Rett as well as hurting him physically, and while his body had mostly healed, Ridge knew that even Malachi had no idea how long it would be for the mental scars to mend.

"What do you mean?" Ridge demanded.

Malachi looked at Rett with an expression Ridge couldn't quite decipher. "As difficult as it is to see him thrash, he's able to give voice to what he's experiencing. Because of the toll the fit takes on his body, he tires quickly. If I give him something to make him sleep more soundly, he loses both an outlet for his pain and a limit on the duration of the vision."

"Shit," Ridge muttered. Enabling Rett to sleep better would be selfish because while doing so would make it easier and less frightening for Ridge, Rett would be plunged even more deeply into the images that troubled him.

"I'm sorry," Malachi replied. "But I sense no danger to his life. I believe the wisest thing is to let the fit run its course. His visions have been true. When they come to him, it's for a reason. I think the best we can do is keep him from hurting himself and see what the vision reveals."

Malachi walked away, leaving Ridge and Rett alone. Rett arched and twisted, muscles tightening so much that the cords of his neck stood out, and his hands clawed, white-knuckled, against the sheet.

"Wake up," Ridge coaxed. "Please, Rett, wake up. We just saved you from the worst of what Letwick and his torturer did. You can't give up now."

Rett dropped back against the bed, in stark contrast to the rictus strain of his muscles just seconds before. He moaned, shivering, although the room was warm.

Ridge drifted off, with his head on the edge of Rett's mattress, one hand locked around his best friend's wrist. He floated in a half-sleep, jerking awake every time Rett twitched.

"Ridge?"

The whispered name roused Ridge. It took a moment, and then he was as awake as if he had jumped into an icy river.

"Are you back?" Ridge asked, unsure whether Rett had woken or whether this was part of yet another scenario in his mind.

"Yeah. Gods—how long?"

Ridge scrubbed a hand over his face to hide the depth of his relief. "About half a candlemark since you went down. The fit lasted for a short while, and you've been out since then."

"Help me up."

Ridge helped Rett sit. Malachi appeared in the doorway with a cup of tea, so he had obviously been listening for Rett to wake.

"Drink this." Malachi passed the cup to Rett. "It will soothe your nerves—and your throat."

Ridge sat back, giving Rett space. Rett sipped the hot tea, collecting his wits.

Probably putting off explaining what he saw for as long as he thinks we'll let him get away with it, Ridge thought.

"I saw a valet at a great house, serving a man I'm sure was a younger version of Duke Letwick." Rett didn't raise his gaze from his tea. "Then a much older version of the servant, working in a grist mill. There was a signpost—I think it said *Dorben*. I saw figures dressed in black fighting in the mill—I knew the miller was in danger. I couldn't see how the fight ended."

"Dorben's Crossing is a market town a few candlemarks' ride from here," Malachi spoke up from where he leaned against the doorframe. "The last I heard, it did have a grist mill."

"You think the miller had some connection with Letwick?" Ridge asked. "Why did someone attack him?"

Rett shook his head. "I don't know—but visions usually leave out the in-between bits. If he worked for Letwick, he might know something about Letwick's missing witch. Maybe we're not the only ones trying to find the witch—and now that Letwick himself is dead, someone is cleaning up loose ends."

"Any idea when this happens?" Malachi asked. Ridge knew that Rett's visions intrigued the necromancer because their magics worked differently.

"What I saw happened indoors, so I couldn't get any idea of the season or time of day, but my visions haven't usually given us much lead time. It could already be too late to save the miller," Rett replied. He moved to stand up, and Ridge laid a hand on his shoulder.

"It's the middle of the night. You've had a bad time of it. Sleep until dawn, and then we'll go find this miller of Dorben's Crossing," Ridge urged.

"There's no time—" Rett protested.

"You're in no condition to ride right now," Malachi said in a voice that didn't leave the topic up for debate. "Kane and Henri can fetch the horses as soon as the sun is up, and I'll have breakfast ready. The miller isn't likely to be at the mill in the middle of the night, early morning will be the busiest time with the most people around—hardly when someone would stage an attack."

Rett glowered but didn't try to get up again, which gave Ridge an idea of just how awful Rett must feel.

"Eat something, drink some more tea, and sleep it off," Ridge suggested, trying to sound reassuring and hoping he hid the depth of his worry. "Henri and I will be in reach if you need anything."

Rett handed back his cup and laid down, moving gingerly as if his head hurt. Ridge knew better than to ask how his partner was feeling. Rett would not admit to anything that might be used to argue him out of leaving the tower.

"I'll bring you broth and bread," Malachi said. "That should set easily on your stomach." Ridge couldn't read the mage's expression well enough to guess whether he remained worried about Rett's recovery.

Henri bustled in shortly afterward with a tray holding a bowl of steaming soup, a glass of water, and several slices of bread with butter. While Henri arranged the tray on the stand next to Rett's bed, Ridge helped Rett sit up and propped him with pillows.

"Eat," Henri ordered, with hands on his hips.

Rett glowered but did as he was told, and Ridge knew his obstinate fellow assassin was much more likely to put up with Henri fussing over him.

Henri smiled at the small victory. Rett seemed to like the taste and ate slowly but steadily.

"Kane and I went to check on the horses this afternoon," Henri told them, plunking himself down cross-legged on the floor. "Wish they weren't stabled so bloody far away."

Ridge raised an eyebrow. "It would give away the charade of Malachi not being able to leave the tower—or have visitors—if there are strange horses milling about, wouldn't it?"

Henri chuckled. "Right you are. Doesn't mean I can't grumble the entire way there and back, just for the sake of hearing myself talk."

"They're all right?" Rett paused, long enough to ask. Ridge knew how much they all cared about their mounts.

"They're fine," Henri replied. "Being spoiled a bit, to tell the truth. The farmer does well by them."

"That's good." Rett had finished his food, but the toll of the fit showed in his face. He looked exhausted, thinner than he should be, with dark circles beneath his eyes making it clear that sleep remained elusive.

Henri hurried to remove the tray and dishes, and Ridge helped Rett lie flat again. "Rest," Ridge told him and saw a flash of stubbornness in Rett's eyes before his body failed to make good on his threat.

"Gods, I hate this," Rett grumbled. "I'm not a prisoner, and Letwick is dead, and it's still not fucking done."

Ridge fought down the guilt that flared at Rett's words, even though he knew there was no way he could have found Rett any sooner. *If I'd searched longer ... if I hadn't given him up for dead ... if I'd have put the clues together more quickly ...*

"Not your fault," Rett muttered as if he sensed the direction Ridge's thoughts had taken. "You did the best you could. And you came for me. Stop second-guessing. You're thinking so loudly it's keeping me awake." The hint of a smile made Ridge finally believe Rett might be getting better.

"I'll go think my loud thoughts in the other room," Ridge teased. "But I'll be back to check on you."

He waited until Rett settled under the blankets before he slipped out to the main room, leaving the door ajar so he would hear if nightmares or another fit troubled Rett's sleep.

In the sitting room, Malachi read a book while Kane and Henri played cards.

"There's a pot on the fire with more soup," Malachi said without looking up when Ridge entered. "Help yourself."

Ridge nodded his thanks and fixed a bowl, sitting near the hearth as he ate. He was surprised at how hungry he was, then remembered that he had been unable to eat more than a few bites at a time while Rett was unconscious.

"This is good," he managed over a mouthful.

Malachi chuckled. "I had to learn to cook for myself or starve. I didn't want to give anyone the satisfaction of getting rid of me so easily."

For a place of confinement, Rune Keep was remarkably comfortable. Then again, its single occupant was a powerful witch and a former advisor to the king. The accommodations not afforded to him by his status were addressed with the clever use of hidden magic.

When he had eaten his fill, Ridge rinsed his bowl and set it aside. "Do you know anything about Dorben's Crossing or the miller?"

Malachi finally looked up from his reading. "An unremarkable place, or so I'm told."

Kane kept his gaze on his hand of cards. "It's a market town. People come and go. Good place for a miller since people either come to town to buy flour or farmers bring their grain to grind. If the miller used to be connected to a noble house, he's hidden it well."

"There's got to be a story there, to go from Letwick's estate to a backwater market town," Henri observed. "It's unusual to leave a position in a noble house. Those roles are often held for a lifetime. Some are inherited." He selected two cards and laid them down, prompting a glower and a muttered curse from Kane.

Henri spoke assuredly as if from personal experience, and Ridge wondered again about their valet's history before he came to them.

"I don't know much about noble houses," Ridge replied. "How does it work, leaving like that?"

"It's rarely by choice," Malachi said, still looking at his book. "Someone can be dismissed for theft, or laziness—or gossiping. Families guard their privacy."

Whether Malachi himself had been born to wealth, he had been a healer and advisor to King Kristoph, with plenty of opportunities to observe the ways of the nobility first-hand.

"Why would someone choose to leave?" Ridge suspected the answer would reveal a lot about the man from Rett's vision.

"Sometimes a person has family responsibilities or bad health. Those are the excuses used as well when someone has a moral disagreement but dares not object," Malachi replied, with a bitterness in his voice that suggested personal experience.

"It takes money to buy a mill," Ridge said.

Malachi shrugged. "Perhaps the valet was thrifty, or maybe he worked out an arrangement with the former owner of the mill. An old man with no heirs might leave his mill to a worker who won his trust. Or perhaps the man in Rett's vision doesn't own the place and merely works there."

Ridge nodded, finding the theories persuasive. "If he was a valet to Letwick, he might know something about the Duke's witch. Anything would be more than what we have now."

"There's no way to know until you talk to him," Henri pointed out as he shuffled the cards. "We have to go."

"I don't like the timing," Ridge protested.

"Doesn't really matter," Kane said never taking his eyes off Henri as the valet shuffled the deck. "Still need to go. Rett's visions are true."

Ridge glanced toward the room where Rett slept. "I know they are. That's what worries me."

"Are you sure you're up for this?" Ridge knew as soon as he spoke that he'd said the wrong thing.

Rett glared at him. "You think I'm not?"

Ridge raised his hands, palms out, in appeasement. "Rett, I didn't mean it that way—"

"Then how did you mean it? It's been a month—"

"Since you almost died," Ridge interrupted.

"We're assassins. Getting hurt goes with the job," Rett snapped.

"You were tortured. They drugged you and used magic. Even with Malachi's power, he wasn't sure he could save you."

"I remember."

"No, you don't. Not all of it," Ridge fussed. "Not the days you wouldn't wake up or when you were lost in your nightmares. But I do. And before you risk getting hurt again, I want to make sure you're not rushing back out there to prove something. Because you don't have to prove anything to me."

Ridge had been despondent when he thought that Rett had died in the explosion that claimed the life of the king. They were brothers-at-arms, bonded by hardship and by the shared secret of their magic.

Rescuing Rett had been an obsession once Ridge found out he was still alive. Together with Henri and Kane, Ridge had managed to find Rett and kill his captors. But Rett had been close to death, body broken and mind potentially shattered by dark magic. Desperate for help, Kane brought them to Malachi. Malachi had agreed to do what he could to heal Rett in exchange for help clearing his name from false charges.

"Maybe I need to prove something to myself," Rett answered. "Malachi doesn't think I'll keel over. The wounds are healed, and the memories are as good as they're going to get. I need to get back out there and work, or I'm going to go crazy. Crazier," he amended with a grimace.

"You're not crazy," Ridge shot back. "And I get that you want out of the tower. Do you remember the last time I broke my leg? I was a lousy patient, and you damn near locked me in the basement to keep me from riding before the bone healed."

Rett smirked. "Yeah. You were a pain in the ass."

Ridge rolled his eyes. "My point being, I wanted to go out before I was ready, and you stopped me. Now I'm returning the favor."

He had lived through weeks of sleepless nights as Rett woke screaming, trapped in memories of his ordeal and hallucinating as the potions used on him gradually waned. Malachi's considerable magic kept Rett alive and reversed as much damage as possible, but some wounds were beyond even his power to heal.

Ridge and Henri had suffered through those weeks along with Rett, never knowing if he would wake from his terrors or become lost in nightmares. Without Malachi's ability as a necromancer to bind soul to body, Rett would have died. Even after he was out of danger, recovery had been slow and painful as Rett regained his strength and clawed his way back to sanity.

Rett shook his head. "It's different, and you know it. I want to work so I don't keep reliving what happened. I need a win, Ridge."

Ridge rubbed a hand over his eyes, willing away a looming headache. "We both do. They've been hard to come by. I just can't take more losses."

King Kristoph was dead without an heir. Yefim Makary, the self-styled Witch Lord and the architect of the plot to kill the king, was still at large, and his sympathizers among the nobility remained a danger to the kingdom. Ridge had a bounty on his head. Associating with him made Henri and Rett outlaws and fugitives as well. Friends and allies had paid dearly for their loyalty. Nearly losing Rett had been the breaking point.

"No guarantee," Rett replied, but his voice lacked the heat from earlier. "I know the tower is a sanctuary, but it's also a cage. Besides, you need me watching your back."

"Kane—"

"Not the same, and you know it."

"It's only been a month," Ridge countered, knowing that he'd already lost.

Rett pounced on the opening. "That's long enough when we've lost track of the Witch Lord, we don't know if Burke and Caralin are still alive, and there's no legitimate heir to the throne."

Burke was the Shadow Master, their ranking officer, and one of the few who had believed them initially about the Witch Lord's potential threat. Many of their fellow assassins resented Ridge and Rett's success, particularly since neither of them came from wealthy or titled families. Caralin had been a trusted ally, if not exactly a friend. Since Kristoph's murder, both Burke and Caralin had vanished, and neither Ridge nor Kane had been able to discover whether they had survived.

"Did you forget that I've got a price on my head? It's not just about doing our jobs—the other Shadows are trying to kill us and so are the Witch Lord's henchmen and the whole godsdamn army," Ridge protested.

"Sounds like a normal week to me." Rett managed a half-smile that Ridge took as an olive branch. "We do what we do better together. Let's get to it. Besides—I'm the one who saw where to go and who to talk to in a vision. You *have* to take me."

"A vision that caused a fit. You don't remember that part," Ridge shot back, eyes wide with worry and face flushed with anger. "I shoved my belt between your teeth so they didn't shatter with the way you were clenching your jaw and throwing yourself around the room. You didn't wake up right away either. I thought you were gone—again."

"Still here," Rett said, spreading his arms wide to demonstrate that fact. "Still alive."

Ridge threw up his hands. "Fine. You win. But if you get hit on the head and undo all of Malachi's healing, I'm going to truss you up and throw you in the dungeon."

"We're hiding out in a magical prison. This *is* the dungeon."

"I'll dig a new level."

Rett shook his head. "That doesn't even make sense." The sharp anger from earlier had eased, replaced by concern. "If this is about getting vengeance, give it up before you get yourself—or both of us—killed. You and Kane already executed Duke Letwick for masterminding Kristoph's murder. The doctor who tortured me is dead. So why—"

"You know there's more to it than that," Ridge argued, although a nagging voice in his mind thought Rett had a point.

"I understand that the kingdom is in chaos, and the Witch Lord is still free, but Ridge, for all we know, we're the last of the Shadows loyal to King Kristoph. There's too much for two men to do."

"Not just two." Ridge lifted his chin, still ready to argue. "We've got Henri, plus Malachi and Kane. Gil and Luc. Maybe Burke and Caralin. Lady Sally Anne and Lorella, plus Sofen and the kids," he said, listing their allies. "And most of us have an extra edge with some magic."

Ridge and Rett had discovered back in the orphanage that they shared the rare ability to see the stain left on a person's soul when they pledged themselves to the service of a dark warlock. Magic of any kind was dangerous knowledge in Landria, likely to result in being conscripted into the army or taken by the priests.

The sound of clapping made them both turn. "Very entertaining," Malachi said from where he leaned against the doorframe. "If you're through with your spat, Henri is downstairs waiting with your horses. Kane said he'd catch up with you in Dorben's Crossing."

Ridge nodded, stuffing down his worry and anger. He needed to be focused and logical. Distraction and emotion could get them all killed. "Thank you," he said. "For everything."

Malachi laughed. "Come back when you're finished. You're safer here than anywhere else, and I've gotten rather used to the company."

Rett murmured his gratitude when he passed by, and Malachi laid a hand on his shoulder. "You're both right, and you're both wrong. You need to get back into the fight before you lose your nerve," he said to Rett before turning back to Ridge. "And you will never be able to keep everyone safe, which is not a failure."

Ridge felt like the witch saw down to his bones. As a child, he had been the only one of his family to survive a fever that swept through his town. Although he had been very young, he remembered doing all that he could to ease their suffering. They died anyway.

Deep down, Ridge knew that colored everything in his life.

"Guess it depends on how you define the word," Ridge replied with a hint of challenge in his voice.

Malachi smiled, taking Ridge's pique in stride like an errant child. "Go. Bring back what you find, and we'll put the pieces together."

Malachi rarely left his tower, even though he had long ago defeated its security spells. As he had explained, he had gotten comfortable there, and if they found out he could leave, they would just imprison him somewhere else. So he remained the hub, researching and scrying while the others put the plans into motion.

"At least the weather favors a ride," Henri observed as they headed toward Dorben's Crossing. The blue sky and mild temperatures teased a return to summer when fall was at the doorstep.

"Enjoy it while it lasts," Rett replied. "It'll be cold soon enough. I'm going to miss the large fireplace in that last safe house," he added, sounding wistful.

"I shall keep that in mind for when we return, and I have to go looking for apartments all over again," Henri replied. "Pity that we had to flee like that. It's going to take twice as long to provision as usual."

Ridge and Rett had learned quickly that their "valet" possessed the knowledge of a seneschal and the street smarts of a cutpurse. He seemed to have contacts everywhere, high-born and vagrant alike, and could acquire just about anything quickly, albeit by dubious means. They'd never gotten a reliable answer about his past, but neither cared to press the matter. Henri was unquestionably loyal, and that was what counted.

"Speaking of which," Henri continued. "I have a list of items Malachi asked me to bring back. While you talk to the contact, I'll take care of business and meet up with you later."

"I wish we knew more about this mysterious connection," Ridge grumbled. "What you saw in your vision didn't give us much to go on. I feel like we're going into this blind."

"We are," Rett replied with a shrug. "Which is how it always works until we figure things out. I saw Duke Letwick, and then I saw a man milling flour and a signpost for Dorben's Crossing. The way the visions work, that means there's a link. How they're linked, I won't know until we talk to him. But if we want to track down Letwick's witch, then we need to follow the clues we get."

Ridge clenched his jaw to avoid an argument. He hoped this trip would be quick and uneventful, which meant he could get Rett back to the safety of Rune Keep and buy more time for him to heal.

"We'll look for the miller, and then we go home. I don't want to push you the first time we're back on the job."

Rett sighed. "All right. I like feeling better. Believe me, I don't want to be flat on the floor again. But I've never had a dream be wrong—or unimportant—even if it didn't make sense at the time."

Ridge looked away, unwilling to concede the point even though he knew Rett was right. He just hoped that whatever Rett's vision led them to was worth the risk.

Dorben's Crossing was a market town at both a crossroads and a river ferry. That made for good trade, and despite the chaos over kings and succession, out here in the country, such things mattered much less than the price of wheat.

Ridge wasn't surprised by the presence of soldiers—market towns meant traders and farmers carrying plenty of coin, which was a magnet for thieves. Before Kristoph's death, Ridge could have flashed one of the king's signed warrants, and the soldiers would have backed off with deep respect.

Although they had altered their appearance, Ridge couldn't afford to let his guard down. The soldiers paid them no heed, but Ridge remained wary. Henri veered off to the apothecary with a promise to meet them at the first crossing outside of town.

The mill was quiet at this time of day. Most farmers came early in the morning, leaving the miller to his work once they sold their grain and picked up their flour.

"Did you see anything else? What would someone connected to Letwick be doing all the way out here?" Ridge asked.

"Hiding, same as us," Rett replied. "If we find him, we can ask."

Ridge had the awful sense that Rett's vision might have left out something important, but it was too late to back down now. He knew how his partner was when he set his mind on something, and Rett was as fixated on tracking this lead as he was on proving himself.

"We're here. Let's get this over with so we can go back."

Rett circled around to the lower door by the river while Ridge headed for the main entrance. He palmed a throwing knife, ready for trouble.

Ridge opened the door cautiously, standing to one side to fend off an attack. He ventured in, and his gaze swept the room. This floor had the hopper for the grain and the two massive millstones. A man looked up, finally noticing Ridge since the clatter of the grinding stones drowned out all other sound.

"Did you come for flour?" the miller shouted above the noise. He was in his middle years, and while his calloused palms and strong arms were the result of hard work, his fine features suggested a more refined past.

"No. I need to ask you some questions about Duke Letwick."

The miller looked down, but not before Ridge saw fear in his eyes. "Don't know who you're talking about."

"We know you're connected to him. Just answer a few questions, and we'll go. We don't want to make trouble for you." Ridge caught a glimpse of Rett coming up the stairs from the lower floor and shifted his position to block the miller's line of sight.

"I told you—I don't know who that is." His anger might have been convincing if his hands weren't shaking.

"Try again." Rett had come up behind Ridge. His voice had gone low and dangerous.

The miller took a step back. "Why? How did you find me?"

"Don't worry—we won't tell anyone where you are," Rett replied, avoiding a direct answer. "Please," he added, softening his tone. "It's important. You could save lives."

The miller swore under his breath. "I was trying to save a life—mine. You need to go."

"Not until you tell us about Letwick," Ridge repeated.

The miller looked from one man to the other and then slumped. "Do you promise you'll go away and leave me alone? I'm no one of importance."

"Then why are you hiding here in a tiny town? Start talking. The sooner you tell us what we want to know about Letwick, the sooner we'll leave," Rett said.

The miller dragged a hand over his face, leaving traces of flour behind. "I was Duke Letwick's valet for twenty years. He wasn't a good man or a nice man, but I had a comfortable position and such things are hard to find."

"What about his witch?" Rett pressed.

The miller's eyebrows shot up. "His witch?"

"I think you know," Ridge replied. "Tell us, and we're done."

"It was never acknowledged that he was a witch," the miller said. "But if you were near him, you could feel it. Even the Duke treated him with care. I could never tell which of them held the upper hand."

"What do you remember?" Rett asked.

"He would come from time to time and talk with the Duke. They would retreat to the parlor all day, taking their meals there. The witch wasn't a large man, and his looks were average, but power surrounded him. All of the servants stayed as far away as they could."

"Can you describe him?" Ridge tried to keep his impatience out of his voice.

"Not particularly tall, dark hair, a face that wouldn't stand out in a crowd. He had a birthmark on his neck. The cook believed it was a sign of an evil spirit. It was easy to spot if he didn't turn up his collar. Blood red, like someone had wrapped fingers around his neck and squeezed."

"And a name?"

"The Duke called him Noxx. I doubt dodgy sorts like him go by their real name," the miller added. As he talked, his eyes darted in one direction and another, looking for threats.

"Do you remember anything else that would help us locate him?" Ridge asked.

The miller looked at him as if he were crazy. "Why would you want to find him? Stay as far away as you can."

"Is he why you left the Duke's employ?" Rett's question must have hit a nerve because the miller's head snapped up.

"I've said too much already," the miller replied. "I left the duke and came here to start over, and I don't need anyone churning up muddy water. Nothing good can come of it."

"Duke Letwick is dead," Ridge said. "He was part of the conspiracy that killed the king. We know his witch was involved. He's missing. He needs to pay for his crimes."

The miller paled and gave a sharp, bitter laugh. "Pay for his crimes? That's rich. His kind never do. I didn't know anything about any plan to harm the king. But I do remember that the witch had no love for him. I got the feeling it was something personal, not just a difference of opinion. Don't know more than that—don't want to know."

"Anything else?" Rett pressed.

The miller shook his head. "No. I've been here for several years—whatever happened after I left isn't my business. I gave you what you wanted. Now, get out."

Ridge and Rett started for the door, then Rett turned back. "We're probably not the only one looking for Noxx. You might want to take precautions."

They rode back the way they came, heading for the place they agreed to meet Henri. Halfway there, Rett swayed in his saddle and groaned, raising one hand to his temples.

"Rett?" Ridge asked, worried.

"We've got to go back to the mill. Something's wrong."

"We're due to meet Henri," Ridge protested, hoping to get Rett back to the tower as soon as possible.

"No. It's important." Rett reined in his horse and turning around, taking off toward the town at a gallop. That forced Ridge to follow, cursing under his breath the whole way.

The mill was quiet when they arrived, looking no different than it had less than a candlemark earlier.

"Are you sure?" Ridge whispered as they secured the horses in the scant protection of a nearby copse of trees.

Rett didn't answer, but he pulled his knife and headed toward the building. Ridge elbowed past him, leading the way while Rett watched behind them.

As soon as they entered the mill, Ridge smelled blood. He glanced at Rett and knew by his expression that he also caught the scent. They moved around the massive grinding apparatus, and Ridge stopped so abruptly that Rett ran into him.

"Damn," Ridge muttered, staring at the miller's body, along with the corpses of two other men he had never seen before.

"Shit," Rett said. "I could swear we weren't followed. And who killed the men who stabbed the miller?"

"Like you told him—other people might have a reason to find Letwick's witch. Someone obviously thought he had important information, but he didn't give us much to work from," Ridge said. "We're compromised. We need to leave *now.*"

"Wait." Rett walked over to the miller's corpse and turned him over, paying no attention to the blood. He searched the dead man's pockets and finally settled for removing a bracelet of woven leather from his left wrist.

"What are you doing?" Ridge hissed as he watched the door, worried that whoever killed the others might return to kill them as well.

Rett pocketed the bracelet. "Resonance," he said. "Maybe we can summon his ghost."

Ridge knew that his partner meant Malachi but dared not speak the outcast mage's name aloud for fear of being overheard.

"Good thinking. Let's go."

A dark shadow dropped from the catwalk over the chute to the millstones, driving Rett to the ground. Before Ridge could go to his aid, a man stepped from among barrels of flour. Ridge found himself facing his Shadow Master, Burke. Caralin dragged Rett to his feet and held a knife against his throat.

"We need to talk," Burke said.

Ridge raised his hands in surrender. "Easy," he urged. "Let's discuss this like colleagues."

Caralin's knife dug against Rett's throat, raising a thin line of blood. Rett didn't struggle, although Ridge knew his partner could fight his way free if he was willing to hurt his captor. Burke and Caralin had been their only allies for so long, Ridge guessed his partner was willing to hear them out, despite the attack.

"Did you kill Kristoph?" Burke leveled a glare at both of them.

"Are you fucking kidding?" Ridge glared back, unamused. "It was the Duke of Letwick, on orders from the Witch Lord."

"Heard you were dead," Caralin remarked. "I guess they got the details wrong."

"Where have you been?" Ridge asked, his voice calm and level, the way it was when he was murderously angry.

"Staying alive," Burke snapped. "Much like the two of you, apparently."

"Did you kill him?" Ridge jerked his head toward the dead miller.

"No. I don't expect you to believe me, but it's the truth. We had been watching the two men who attacked him," Burke replied. "Didn't know what their plan was or who they intended to meet, but they had links to Letwick, and we got suspicious when they suddenly left their hiding place and went on the road. So we followed."

"We got here too late to save the miller," Caralin said. "Then they attacked us, and there wasn't much time for conversation."

"Who sent the Shadows after us?" Ridge demanded. "They tried to kill us. They're still hunting us."

"They're hunting us too. Orders from the palace. You and Rett might have been framed for Kristoph's death, but they put out the word we were in on it. None of those loyal to Kristoph are safe until the Witch Lord is stopped."

"Let him go." Ridge leveled a look at Burke and glanced to Caralin. "Drop the knife."

Burke nodded, and Caralin eased up on her hold. Rett moved to stand beside Ridge and gave a nod of assurance that he was all right.

"Whatever you think you know is wrong," Ridge said.

"Oh, really?" Burke mocked. "Start talking. I want to know everything."

Ridge and Rett took turns quickly telling shortened versions of their stories about the day King Kristoph died. Together, their tales wove a fairly complete picture, even though they had been separated for parts of it. They left out anything to do with Kane and Malachi or the ghosts. Burke and Caralin listened in silence as the two assassins talked.

"And then we ran," Ridge finished. He raised his head defiantly. "Where the fuck were you?"

Burke met his gaze. "Hunted," he replied. "When the building came down on Kristoph—and Rett—we realized the game would flip. We could stay and die, and the truth would die with us. We thought that both of you were dead. So we got away and kept going."

"We've been quietly gathering information since we left the city," Caralin said. "Anything we could find about Kristoph and the Witch Lord that we didn't already know—talking to old associates, schoolmates, teachers. We weren't even sure what we were looking for, but we thought we might stumble on something useful."

"And did you?" Rett glared at Caralin, clearly not ready to forgive the shallow cut on his throat that still bled.

"Maybe," she replied. "Rumor has it that Kristoph sired a bastard when he was in his teens. Seems to have been kept quiet at the time, so not many people knew. The one who told us also said the child was born dead, but that seems a little too convenient."

Ridge caught his breath. "You think there's an heir?"

Burke shrugged. "Worth looking into. Did you learn anything from the miller?"

Ridge shared what little the man had told them. "It's not much, but it's more than we had before."

"Noxx?" Burke murmured. "I think I've heard that name, but I can't remember where."

"Glad you're alive, nice to catch up, but we really need to go," Ridge said, knowing that Henri would be worried and feeling too exposed.

"We knew Ridge was alive when we heard about the warrant," Caralin replied. "And for the record—we didn't really think you'd killed the king. But we had to ask."

"Take care of yourselves—and be careful," Rett said. "And the next time, you don't have to attack to get our attention."

Ridge and Rett left first, and despite the collaborative end to their run-in with Burke and Caralin, neither turned their back on their former colleagues. They took a longer, circuitous route but didn't see or sense anyone following.

As Ridge expected, Henri was pacing when they arrived late to the rendezvous point. The cut on Rett's neck immediately drew his attention. "You were attacked?"

"Friendly misunderstanding," Ridge replied, through gritted teeth, still annoyed at Caralin for injuring Rett.

"We'll tell you everything—but not here," Rett said, swinging up to his saddle. "Let's go home."

Chapter Three

Edvard the ghost was waiting when they returned to Rune Keep.

"He showed up not long after you went to town," Malachi told them with a shrug as if it were the most normal thing in the world—and maybe for a necromancer, it was.

Rett was more exhausted than he had let on to Ridge and Henri. But he could hear spirits, while Ridge could not. Begging off would reveal just how far from recovered Rett remained. He couldn't bear to disappoint Ridge again or risk anyone thinking he wasn't up to the hunt.

"It will save a lot of repeating things if I make it possible for everyone to hear Edvard," Malachi said as if he guessed Rett's dilemma. Rett managed a grateful smile for the necromancer.

"You've come a long way to see us," Rett greeted the ghost as Malachi brought out a pot of tea and cups for all of the mortals, and they sat around the table. "It must be important."

He and Ridge had met Edvard when they were working to break a smuggling ring. The ghost had helped them by being their spy and messenger, and when the situation was over, Edvard stayed. He said he wanted to keep helping, and Lorella, a powerful medium who had assisted Ridge and Rett on several occasions, found a way to make that possible.

Edvard haunted a coin that Rett usually kept in his pocket. At first, he and Lorella had sent the coin back and forth by messenger to send Edvard with news. Then they hit on the idea of having Edvard haunt two coins and move between them, which made sharing information much faster.

"Sofen and the others like him are using their abilities to listen for chatter about the Witch Lord," Edvard said. "Makary is shielding himself, so we don't know where he is. But he has people doing his bidding at the palace and elsewhere. He still wants to control the throne, but when you killed Letwick, it fouled his plans. He's looking for another way. Trust nothing from the palace."

"Nothing new there," Ridge muttered.

"With the Duke of Letwick gone, and his younger brother missing, the succession is unclear again," Rett replied. "Have they put forth another possible candidate?"

"Not that Sofen or the others were able to see. They also have not heard of any more stolen children, and it has been a while since new children have found their way to Harrowmont," Edvard told them.

Lady Sally Anne was the mistress of Harrowmont, a fortified castle. She survived an abusive husband—and may have hastened his demise—and then turned the lands and great house into a place of sanctuary for abused women and children with psychic abilities. Lorella had taken refuge there. So had Sofen and other orphans with a forbidden touch of magic whom Ridge and Rett had freed from slavers and the Witch Lord's supporters.

"Lady Sally Anne and Lorella—are they well?" Rett asked. He and Ridge appreciated Lorella's friendship and support, and Lady Sally Anne was a patron with valuable—if secretive—connections.

"Yes. They send their regards. The siege has kept them busy."

Ridge looked up sharply. "Siege?"

"Duke Foster, under the Witch Lord's sway, has sent troops to attack Harrowmont," Edvard said. "They fight under false colors since Foster is too much a coward to have them carry his crest into battle."

"Is Harrowmont defended?" Ridge asked.

Edvard chuckled. "Oh, yes. If the soldiers thought it would be an easy fight, they were mistaken. The women without magic pour out the chamber pots onto the attackers' heads or boil dirty wash water and tip the cauldrons onto any foolish enough to get close. The children throw rocks and launch volleys of arrows. Sofen and those with magic send boils, lice, dysentery, and rats to plague the encampment, or work small spells to break equipment, frighten horses, and attract lightning and floods."

"Duke Foster must be paying well for them to put up with conditions like that," Kane said, with a grin that made it clear he relished the abuse heaped on the besieging troops. "And using natural means makes it difficult for a charge of witchcraft to stick. The commander just looks exceedingly unlucky."

"What else?" Rett asked. Malachi was lending Edvard some of his magic to remain visible as well as audible to the others, making such a long conversation much less cumbersome than if Rett had to relay every question and answer.

"Lorella has been experimenting with using coins like mine to attract spirits to Harrowmont," Edvard replied. "Most of us can't travel far on our own without an anchor. Lorella and the witches have figured out how to use two coins to create a pathway for the ghosts to find their way to sanctuary while keeping out vengeful spirits."

"Why do ghosts need sanctuary?" Malachi frowned.

Edvard looked uncomfortable. "What remains of us—consciousness and memory—is energy. Some of the Witch Lord's followers can drain living people and ghosts to enhance their own power."

Rett had never seen a ghost look frightened before, but Edvard clearly feared that fate.

"Is it working?" Malachi took the situation seriously and sounded angry at the desecration.

"Yes, according to what Lorella has learned," Edvard replied. "Of course, the ghosts are grateful for protection and are more than willing to haunt the attacking troops, provided they have no witches among them."

"Those sorry bastards don't understand who they're dealing with," Ridge said, shaking his head in respect for Lady Sally Anne's strategy. "Anyone who thought they'd be an easy win for being 'mere' women and children is going to have his balls handed to him on a platter."

"When a break in the siege permits, Sofen and the other psychics search for Brother Tom and Green Knoll. So far, without success," Edvard continued. "Anything the ghosts are able to report that pertains to the Witch Lord's plans, Lorella passes on to Gillis Arends, through messengers like me."

"We don't want to put you in danger of getting drained," Rett said, alarmed. He had grown fond of their ghostly companion. And while worrying about a ghost's "death" seemed odd, Rett didn't want their friend to vanish.

"I want Landria to be rid of the Witch Lord and his followers. This is my way to help. I'm in far less danger than a mortal messenger. It gives me purpose," Edvard explained.

"Thank you. We've gotten used to having you with us. It would be nice to have you stick around," Ridge put in.

"We will continue to search," Edvard assured them. "And keep you informed." He blinked out, and Malachi leaned back in his chair.

"I figured it was easier to have Edvard speak to all of us at once," Malachi said. He didn't add that it would be less of a drain on Rett, for which Rett was grateful.

Rett felt the fatigue from the day's events crash down. He managed to stay awake during supper and listened more than contributed to the conversation as Ridge retold their encounter with the miller and the unexpected arrival of Burke and Caralin.

Ridge shot him a worried look, but Rett smiled and shook his head, hoping he hid just how bone-deep his tiredness went.

"Do you believe Burke?" Malachi asked.

Ridge shrugged. "As much as I believe anyone—other than you four," he said with a nod to Kane, Henri, Malachi, and Rett. "Burke always had our back—even when he had to work around the king to do it. I think he's telling the truth."

"And the Shadows that were trying to kill you the night we fled to the tower?" Kane asked, clearly not in a forgiving mood.

"If Burke and Caralin are fugitives, the other Shadows are trying to kill them as well," Rett replied. "They never cared for Ridge and me because we showed them up. Caralin didn't take shit from anyone. And Burke told them what to do. No surprise that if the rest of the Shadows saw a way to get rid of all of us that they wouldn't take it—especially if someone played to their egos."

"I hope you're right," Kane said. "I have even less faith in people than you do."

The afternoon sun warmed his cloak and made him sweat beneath his hat, making Rett wish he dared remove the clothing that was part of his disguise. With both the guards and the Shadows looking for them, traveling posed a danger. But the message from Gil requesting they meet with Luc made the risk worthwhile.

"Gil and Malachi are in something of the same situation, aren't they?" Ridge asked Kane as they rode.

"Gil isn't 'imprisoned' the way Malachi is, but he's under surveillance—and Luc is supposed to be watching him," Kane replied. "Although now that Kristoph is dead, I'm not sure that either sentence is in full effect. Gil slips out when necessary, but he's careful not to do it often. He and Luc have worked the situation to their advantage, the same way Malachi and I adapted. It would be inconvenient to have someone notice and change things."

Rett understood the need for meeting far enough from the city to reduce the risk of running into guards and with sufficient distance to avoid attracting attention to Rune Keep. Still, he chafed at the exposure, although he was grateful to be included. Henri had stayed behind to help Malachi, and Rett was determined to prove that he'd healed enough to be on duty again.

"What did you make of Edvard's report on the siege?" Ridge asked Kane.

"More proof that without a strong king, the nobility starts to fight amongst itself," the spy answered. "Raising a private army, sending it without provocation against another noble's lands, and fielding troops to fight without flag or crest? No king would dare allow that to go unchallenged."

"Unless chaos is the whole idea." Rett was disturbed at the suspicions that crossed his mind. "The longer the kingdom goes without naming a new king, the more aggressive the nobles are likely to become—especially the young ones who were open to the Witch Lord's sedition. The older lords loyal to Kristoph fought enough wars beside his father to dampen their appetite for more. The upstarts might see an opportunity to grab as much as they can while there's no one on the throne to stop them."

"That's cynical enough to be possible," Kane allowed. "And we already know the Witch Lord is an opportunist. I have to admit—I'm worried about what Luc has to tell us that's important enough to meet in person. It can't be anything good."

Luc Merchand's position as sheriff gave him the ability to travel without being stopped by the guards. He usually stayed close to the city as Gil's partner in crime-solving, but that freedom to travel came in handy on occasion.

They met at dusk behind the burned hulk of a ruined inn. Luc was waiting for them, standing behind a broken fence that gave him a good view of the road without revealing himself. He held the reins for his bay mount as if ready to make a quick exit if necessary.

"Good to see you again," Kane said, clasping arms with the sheriff. Ridge and Rett followed with a similar greeting.

"Glad to see you're all alive. You know how rumors fly."

"Actually, we don't—we've been out of circulation for a while," Ridge said. Gil and Luc were among the few who knew he and the others had taken shelter with Malachi.

"Right," Luc said, rubbing his palms together. "Gil says that the gossip he hears is evenly split between believing you're both dead—causes vary—and that Rett died in the explosion at Sommerelle while you were spirited away by dark magic."

"Glad we're still keeping them guessing," Rett replied, figuring that gallows humor was better than none at all.

Luc glanced toward the road; Kane had positioned himself to watch for intruders as well, and all four men were well armed. "I've got plenty to tell you, so listen carefully. Gil says that a regency council is being formed to administer the duties of the king by committee until a legitimate heir can be found. That wouldn't be so bad if it were likely to be filled with the nobles known to be loyal to Kristoph."

He paused. "But the younger nobility—the ones who liked the Witch Lord's bluster—are causing problems, and Gil suspects that those in charge of naming the council members have been threatened. Nothing's final yet, but the names being floated as possibilities are not promising."

He handed over a handwritten list, which Ridge slipped into an inside pocket of his coat.

"As for finding the real name for the witch known as Noxx, Gil's sources say he is Georg Hardin, whose mother is the sister of the late, unlamented Duke Letwick, which makes him the duke's nephew."

"Good to know," Rett replied, "but where is he?"

"That's harder to track down," Luc said, licking his lips nervously. "Clearly, Georg—Noxx—doesn't want to be found. Can't blame him since while the duke and the Witch Lord planned the king's death, Noxx's magic bewitched the bombers. Now the duke is dead, and Noxx must know or suspect that you two are alive and out for vengeance."

"Is he still in Landria?" Rett asked.

"Gil thinks so. The Witch Lord may have cultivated the support of certain foreign parties, but Noxx isn't important enough to have done the same. Gil's tracking spell showed

Noxx at Letwick's river home, near Haverford." He snorted. "By the Duke's standards, it's a fishing cabin. By anyone else's measure, it's a small mansion."

Ridge shot a look at Rett. "It's only fitting since I executed the duke at his hunting cabin."

Luc pinched the bridge of his nose. "I didn't hear that."

"I pinned up Kristoph's final writ of execution over Letwick's bleeding corpse. Didn't exactly make a secret of who finished him," Ridge replied.

"That makes it a sanctioned kill," Kane said with a grin. "So your virtue as sheriff remains intact."

"My 'virtue' hasn't been intact for a long time," Luc retorted. "You can blame Gil."

"More than I needed to know," Kane replied, rolling his eyes.

"Getting back to business," Luc said, clearing his throat, "Gil's been asking around about the mage who served King Renvar, Kristoph's father. His real name was Aldridge Morrison, although he went by 'Runcian.' As far as Gil can find out, Aldridge—Runcian—wasn't of noble birth. He was extraordinarily talented and gained the king's notice."

"Everyone always thinks that's a good thing, but it rarely turns out that way in the long run," Rett said.

"True enough," Luc replied. "Runcian served King Renvar for over twenty years. But then, something went wrong. Runcian disappeared, King Renvar was furious, and after that, the royal witches no longer had the same status or level of trust. Renvar turned on magic users and either conscripted them or forced them into hiding. Kristoph continued that policy."

"Interesting," Ridge mused. "Gil doesn't know what the feud was about?"

Luc shook his head. "Not so far. There may not have been witnesses, or Gil might not have asked the right person yet. After all, it was twenty-five years ago, give or take."

"Getting back to Noxx—Gil thinks he's at Letwick's river house?" Rett asked, needing to be certain.

"That's what Gil and I have put together from sources—including some of Gil's ghostly informants," Luc clarified. "I had two reasons for meeting in person—to give you the list and to pass along this." He produced a small, cloth-wrapped bundle from inside his coat, a package that fit in the palm of his hand.

Ridge took it gingerly, unwilling to look inside. "What is it?"

"A ring that belonged to Noxx. After you got Rett out of that fortress where Letwick tortured him, I scouted the area to see if Gil and I could figure out where Noxx had been living. He didn't stay inside the fort, but he had to be nearby to provide Letwick and his torturer with the items they needed," Luc replied.

"I found a small house at the edge of the property that might have been a sentry post at one time," he continued. "Noxx must have left in a hurry because he left behind plenty of witchy evidence. I collected what was left, then cleansed the area the way Gil taught me. When I brought back the stuff Noxx abandoned, Gil said the ring would be the best link to him. Probably took it off when he was mixing ingredients."

Ridge looked at the bundle skeptically. "Is it magic?"

Luc shook his head. "No. Gil was clear on that. But because it was worn on the body, the ring should have a close connection to Noxx. Malachi can weave a spell with the ring as an anchor that can help you bind Noxx—at least until you can get close enough to knock him out or kill him."

"Thanks." Rett eyed the bundle as if it were a serpent. "That should be helpful."

"Just be careful," Luc warned. "Noxx is desperate—and he's a powerful witch. Even though Gil and I did our best to verify, it's very likely to be a trap. Noxx won't just be waiting around to be captured."

"We always assume the worst," Ridge assured him. "That's a big reason why we're still alive."

They thanked Luc again, sent their greetings to Gil, and headed in the opposite direction from the sheriff, back to Rune Keep.

"What do you make of all that?" Ridge asked Kane.

"I trust Luc and Gil. They're telling the truth—as far as they know it," Kane replied. "I don't think Gil would go to the trouble of sending Luc to us if he wasn't sure the information was solid."

"How do we fight a witch?" Rett asked. "It's not safe to take Malachi with us. Even if Noxx really is at the river house, he's sure to have protections. We aren't going to just stroll in and capture him. He'll fight with magic, not swords. I want to make him pay for what he did—but I'd like for us to live through it."

"Malachi will know," Kane said with confidence. "He's fought other witches and won. If we can take Edvard with us to spy, that would help a lot. We'll figure it out."

"Soul magic," Malachi said, holding up the ring in the lamplight for a better look.

"I don't understand—" Rett protested.

Malachi lowered the ring and looked at Rett. "Every magic has an offensive and defensive side to it. You can see ghosts, and they can hear you. But you can also call those spirits who are in range for help, information, or protection. Ghosts are an echo of the soul. If you use your magic to call to Noxx's soul, it will force him to shift his attention to hold himself together, and giving his spirit a good *yank* is disorienting, to say the least."

Rett's hand splayed over his heart on reflex at the thought. "*Disorienting* seems a bit mild."

Malachi chuckled. "I don't think you have the strength to kill like that, but it's a move that certainly costs your opponent precious time recovering. Like a psychic hit to the nuts."

Rett looked dismayed. "It seems like a cheap shot."

Kane shrugged. "So is kicking a fellow in the plums or poking his eyes—but in a fight, you do what you have to do."

"Don't feel discouraged about 'small' magic," Malachi said. "Throwing a rock can kill an enemy just as dead as running him through with a sword. The trick is to use what you have to your best advantage. Doing that with limited power or arcane knowledge requires creativity—but it also means your opponent won't be expecting whatever you throw at him."

"Is there an offensive angle to our Sight?" Ridge asked, glancing between Rett and Malachi.

"Beyond letting you avoid close contact with those who bear the stain? That's a good question," Malachi replied. "Your Sight protects you by letting you see who has bound themselves to dark magic. With training, I think you might learn to use that stain against the person to distract or temporarily cripple them. I'll have to think more about that."

He looked back to the ring. "This has no special magic, but it's old—probably an heirloom, worn for sentimental value. Because of that, there is a resonant bond that comes from close contact with the body over a long period of time."

Malachi passed Noxx's ring back to Rett. "Hold onto the ring when you call to his soul. That bond will strengthen the magic's connection."

"What's the plan if we actually catch Noxx?" Kane leaned against the wall. "We can't bring him back here, so taking him prisoner is out of the question. Question and kill him?"

"Works for me," Ridge replied, and Rett heard the cold tone his partner's voice took when meting out justice became personal.

Malachi glided to another table in his work area and pulled a small stoppered bottle from a box. He handed it to Kane. "If you want to question a witch, you can't just tie him up. You'll need to blunt his magic temporarily as well. I figured this sort of situation would come up, so I created that potion. Put it on a dart or the blade of a knife, and even a small amount will incapacitate."

The look shared between Malachi and Kane underscored the amount of trust the witch had in his partner. "I'll keep it safe," Kane promised.

Malachi turned back to the others. "I've already spoken to Edvard, and he's eager to join you. Not only can he help suss out traps, but if there are local ghosts, he can recruit them to help. Since we don't know much about the sort of magic Noxx wields or how powerful he is, you're going to have to make a lot of this up as you go."

"Just be careful," Malachi said. "You know that Noxx has no hesitation about using his magic to kill and torture. He won't be unprotected, and he's certain to put up quite a fight."

"We'll be ready," Ridge assured the witch, although privately, Rett had doubts.

Even before the Karnon River came into view the next morning, Rett smelled the unmistakable mix of marshland, mud, and fish. Letwick's river house looked like a great home from a bygone era, probably inherited and made into a fishing retreat since Letwick had no interest in the shipping trade.

Edvard scouted the approach from the road to the house and returned to share his report.

"He says that the lane itself is clear, but he sensed magical 'tripwires' along the way and in the brush on either side," Rett reported to the others who couldn't hear or see Edvard easily without magical assistance.

"Any idea what they do?" Kane asked.

Rett listened to Edvard's reply, then shook his head. "No. But it's doubtful they'd be troublesome to ghosts."

"How about closer in?" Ridge asked. "Wardings or traps around the house itself?"

"Nothing substantial," Rett relayed from Edvard. "He says it feels like Noxx threw up whatever he could in a hurry, but there's no old magic guarding the house or grounds."

Kane nodded. "Sounds logical if Noxx is on the run, squatting in his dead master's fishing retreat. He might not expect us to come after him, so he's cautious but not feeling hunted. Yet," he added with a smile that showed his teeth.

"It didn't worry him enough to build a fence," Ridge observed. "Although maybe he didn't want to draw attention to the fact that someone was living here by making changes."

Rett turned back to Edvard and the dozen or so restless ghosts he had rallied to their cause. Some had been Letwick's servants, while others were Noxx's victims. None of the spirits had qualms about helping them get past the traps to settle the score with the dark witch.

"Ready?" he asked the ghosts. Edvard nodded. *"Then let's get going."*

Edvard and the other spirits fanned out across the approach to the river house. Rett followed them, with Kane and Ridge grudgingly bringing up the rear. Other than the rush of water and the rustling of leaves, the area was quiet.

Rett eyed the old house skeptically. Despite the techniques he had discussed with Malachi, he'd never gone up against another witch directly before. Rett hoped that the ghosts could provide a distraction as well as identify any magical traps, giving him a chance to put his own abilities to the test.

Thanks to Edvard and the band of revenants, Rett and the others navigated around the arcane alarms scattered across the grounds and pathway. Without the spirits' help, he knew they would have blundered into several of the spells, alerting anyone in hearing distance. Several of the traps were intended to injure or maim, and Rett felt doubly grateful that the ghosts were able to trip the triggers without harm, making their retreat path all the safer.

Their approach was neither silent nor stealthy, yet no response came from inside the house. As they neared the building, Rett expected Noxx to blast them with winds or send bolts of fire crackling toward them.

When they closed the distance, Rett looked to Edvard. *"Can you see inside? Or go through the walls?"*

Edvard shook his head. *"No. The stone has too much iron in it. We dissipate. I'm sorry."*

Rett watched for movement at the windows, anything that might indicate a magical or mundane defense. The persistent stillness and silence ratcheted up his worry.

"Can you sense anything inside? Or pick up Noxx's whereabouts?"

Edvard paused, concentrating. *"There is a living being inside. I can't tell more details because of the iron in the stone."*

"Ask the ghosts to be ready to help," Rett instructed Edvard. *"We get a door open, I'm counting on you to surround Noxx and form a barrier so he can't just lash out and kill all of us. You just need to give us a chance to get in the first shot."*

"We will do our best," Edvard assured Rett.

With his heart thudding, Rett advanced. The river house was solidly built but in need of repair. He wondered how long it had been since Letwick had visited and whether his heirs would bother to do so. The gray stone offered protection against storm winds and overflowing banks.

Did the builders know the iron content in the walls would keep out ghosts, or was that just a lucky side effect?

As far as they knew, Noxx had no abilities as a medium. If so, that gave Rett and his companions an advantage. *Then again, we have no idea what types of magic he can harness, so I'll hold off on counting the ghosts as a win until it's over.*

No light shone from inside. The dark windows stared down on them, and while Rett strained to see the interior or catch a glimpse of a face or body moving within the building, the reflection of the windowpanes denied him certainty.

Ridge and Kane headed up the front steps, with Rett just a few strides behind. Ridge had a matchlock, while Kane had his bow and arrows with poisoned tips.

The large door swung inward. Then, in the gloom, something stirred.

The creature that lurched from the shadows was unlike anything Rett had seen before. It moved as fast as a running man, but while the body had the same general shape as a person, everything about it felt wrong. From the deathly pallor of the skin to the glazed eyes and the unnatural gait, Rett knew on instinct that the creature wasn't *alive* in the same way they were.

Kolvry, he had a split second to think before it moved toward them, arms outstretched and mouth open, slowed but not stopped by their ghost allies. *Nearly dead people possessed by ghosts.* He had heard of the creatures but never encountered one before.

Ridge fired the matchlock and hit his target, but it kept on coming. Kane's arrows didn't slow it down, although the poison should have felled a large man.

Rett reacted on instinct, knowing that the ghosts couldn't hold back the *kolvry* for long. He narrowed his concentration to the center of the creature's torso and *pulled.*

The monster gave a hoarse cry and shuddered to a stop, limbs flailing. Its form trembled as if fighting against a power it could not shake loose.

Just as Rett felt a thrill of triumph at having stopped the threat, he realized that there was a second *kolvry* waiting in the shadows.

Ridge and Kane closed ranks, exchanging the bow and gun for long knives. Edvard and the ghosts drew together, harrying and blocking the creatures.

One of the monsters moved fast enough to get inside Ridge's reach. It slashed at him with its long nails and hurled him down the steps. The other creature lunged at Kane, teeth bared for a fight.

Whether the creatures could infect Ridge and Kane with a bite or scratch, Rett didn't know, but he moved to shield his friends from the attack. He felt the ghost inside the *kolvry* respond to his magic and tugged again. Fearing for his friends, he doubled his focus and *pulled* at the possessing ghosts with all his might.

Rett tasted blood on his lips. His head throbbed, and his eyes ached. He panted for breath, and his Sight burned like fire at the creatures wholly given to the command of the dark witch.

Something yielded to his magic—a dark, sullied primal energy. Desperate to save Ridge and Kane, Rett ripped the energy free of its moorings and flung it as far as he could.

In his peripheral vision, Rett saw the creatures collapse, motionless heaps on the ground.

A breath later, his vision blurred, and he dropped to his knees, then fell to the side, laboring for breath.

"Rett!" Ridge's voice seemed far away, but Rett felt a hand grip his shoulder tightly and shake him. "Come on, wake up. Kane, he's bleeding from his nose and ears. We've got to get him out of here!"

Rett knew he should feel more worried, given Ridge's frantic tone. Ridge's fingers dug into his upper arm, tight enough to bruise, but the feeling had started to fade as everything around him grew dim.

"Stay with us," Ridge begged.

Rett wanted to tell him that everything would be all right, although he very much doubted that was true. But he couldn't find his voice, let alone draw breath, and he thought his fever might scald his body from the inside.

His muscles seized and he went rigid. Rett's back arched, and his hands formed fists tight enough to dig his fingernails into his palms.

Ridge cursed and then a minute later, wedged a folded belt between Rett's teeth.

"Kane! He's having another fit!" Ridge sounded sick with worry.

I stopped the creatures, saved you and Kane. But I might have gone too far ...

The world around Rett went black.

"Rett?"

Rett heard his name called but couldn't place the voice. It wasn't deep enough or worried enough to be Ridge. He didn't immediately remember what he'd been doing right before waking up, but he felt certain that he hadn't decided to nap on the floor.

"Come on—wake up," the voice begged. "Shit—I'm never going to be able to explain this to the healer."

Rett opened his eyes to stare up at a panicking Brother Tom. Tom sat back on his haunches and sighed in relief.

"Thank the heavens. You're alive."

As consciousness returned, so did pain. Rett's head throbbed, his jaw ached from clenching, and he winced from a pulled muscle in his back. He groaned as he forced himself to sit up. "Do you have willow tea?"

Tom grinned. "I do. And I also have some mighty fine whiskey that we distill right here at Green Knoll. Both are good for what ails you."

Rett managed a weak smile in return. "Tea first, then maybe I'll take you up on the whiskey."

He looked around and realized he was in what was probably Tom's room. "Please tell me I didn't just show up on your floor."

"I found you in the middle of the hallway. I couldn't just leave you there. Had to drag you to my room. I didn't want anyone else to find you," Tom admitted. "Stay here while I get the tea. I'll be right back."

He left the room, and Rett hauled himself into the only chair, leaving the bed for Tom to sit on when he returned. He looked around the monk's cell, surprised to find it not as austere as he expected. A colorful mural adorned one wall, a sunset over a field filled with flowers.

Tom said that no one goes beyond the compound. I wonder how much space that really is?

Tom returned quickly with a steaming mug, and Rett took it and cradled it between his palms, inhaling the familiar scent.

"We keep a kettle brewing with it nearly all the time—helps with the aches and pains that come with working on the farm," Tom told him. "If you decide you want the whiskey, I keep a jug here in the room," he confided with a conspiratorial grin.

"Thank you," Rett said, sipping the hot drink and willing it to ease the discomfort that came with soul traveling. He saw Tom watching him and realized that the monk looked more tired and worn than the previous time he had popped into the monastery. Shadows beneath his eyes and a worried expression made Rett wonder what was going on.

"Has something gone wrong?"

"Have you seen the omens where you come from?" Tom seemed earnest and frightened.

Rett raised an eyebrow. "What kind of omens? When did they start?"

Tom stood and paced the small room. "Just since your last visit. We've felt tremors in the ground. Not enough to cause damage, at least, not yet. But if they get worse, it could be dangerous. We've had more storms of late, worse than usual with wind and lightning, and there's a large black crow that's suddenly taken to sitting on the fence post right outside the kitchen door."

Tom shook his head. "None of that is normal. Brother Kendrick has advised us all to meditate and pray to the gods for wisdom and deliverance, but I fear he doesn't know the cause of the omens."

"What do the others say when Kendrick isn't listening?" Rett cursed his pounding headache, feeling sure something important eluded him.

"They say that it feels like the world might come apart," Tom replied. "I don't think I'm the only one with nightmares, although no one speaks of it."

"What do you dream? It might be important," Rett urged.

"Jumbled things that don't make a lot of sense," Tom said. "A shadow chases me down the hallway. I know that I can't let it catch me, but I never see what it is. In another dream, the outer wall around the compound cracks, and dark water floods inside. I can't get away, and it pulls me under."

He shook his head. "There have been a couple more, but they're much the same. Bad things happen."

Rett frowned, knowing that the dreams mattered and that the threat Tom sensed was not an idle one. "Have you looked for any books about dreams in the library? They might help."

Tom nodded. "I found one that claimed dreams like that were messages, that someone means to cause me trouble, even if I don't see the danger at the moment. But how can that be right? We never leave the compound. No one new has ever come here, except you. And you haven't tried to hurt me."

"I won't hurt you," Rett promised. "I'm not sure why I keep showing up, but I don't mean you harm, and I'll protect you if I can."

"I don't like to sleep anymore," Tom said, and Rett could see the strain in the man's features. "I can tell that some of the others must also get the dreams because we're doing our chores in a daze. I thought Kendrick would say something about it. I think he knows. Maybe he dreams, too."

"Keep looking in the library. I have a feeling the answer is in there, somewhere," Rett told him. The willow tea had taken the edge off his sore muscles. But as he set his empty cup aside, a new sensation stole over him, one he recognized from before.

"Not now, dammit!" Rett muttered. He felt less and less solid as if he were becoming transparent and weightless and might just float away.

"Rett, it's happening again," Tom started toward him as if he meant to grab Rett and anchor him, but before that could happen, everything faded, and Rett felt himself slipping back into unconsciousness.

CHAPTER FOUR

Rett woke up in his bed at Rune Keep, with Ridge asleep in a nearby chair. Rett lay still for a moment, mentally cataloging how he felt. His head still ached, although less since Tom's willow bark tea. The sharp pain of having a pulled back muscle made it clear that the fit had not been imagined.

Next, he turned his attention to assessing Ridge. He remembered the chaos of the fight with the *kolvry* and how he overdrew his limited magic to keep the creatures away from Kane and Ridge.

Clearly, he had been successful only in part since there were fresh bandages on Ridge's right arm and a new bulkiness beneath his shirt that made Rett suspect more wrapping on a shoulder wound.

"Glad to have you back," Ridge said, opening his eyes. Rett figured that Ridge had somehow known he was watching for a few minutes.

"Good to be here. How bad did those *things* get to you and Kane?" Rett asked, worried.

"No one lost an arm or too much blood—although it was a pain in the ass dragging you back to the horses with you out cold and Kane and me with only two good arms between us," Ridge grumbled. Rett knew that beneath the complaint lay relief that they had all returned alive.

"Glad we went in with as much preparation as we did," Rett added. "We were worried about it being a trap—and it was."

"More than you know." Ridge got up and stretched, and Rett wondered how long his friend had spent in the chair, waiting for him to wake. "Either we did something to attract the attention of the guards, or Noxx was able to send them after us. I don't think we would have gotten away from them if the ghosts hadn't spooked their horses." Ridge fixed him with a glare. "Which was harder than usual since you were out cold."

Rett sighed. "Thanks for not leaving me."

"We thought about it—but decided Edvard would never forgive us," Ridge joked. "Seriously—you gave us a scare. You had blood running down your face, you were white as a sheet, and you nearly stopped breathing. Scared the shit out of me."

Rett massaged his temples, hoping the headache would fade. "I didn't know if the magic Malachi and I figured out would work on the *kolvry*. It did—but I had to pull harder than I expected. Then you and Kane got hurt, and I tried as hard as I could."

"The *kolvry* were still alive," Ridge said, meeting Rett's gaze. "Edvard confirmed that. Living men—what was left of them after Noxx tortured them past sensibility and forced ghosts into them."

Rett suddenly couldn't breathe. *That could have been me. I might have ended up like that if Letwick and Noxx had their way.* Memories of the drugs and torture—and dark magic—that he had endured slammed to the forefront, and Rett swayed, dizzy, as his lungs struggled for air.

"Hey, hey, hey! Rett. Breathe!" Ridge grabbed him by the shoulders and gave a shake. "You're safe. Duke and Doctor are dead. We didn't kill Noxx this time, but we will. I swear we will. He'll pay for what he did to you—and to the others. But you've got to breathe."

Rett concentrated on the feel of Ridge's fingers digging into his muscles, grounding him in the present. He focused on the aroma of venison stew and baking bread coming from the keep's small kitchen and the low murmur of voices beyond the bedroom door.

Ridge pressed a glass of whiskey into his hand and guided it to Rett's lips. "Drink. It'll help."

Rett took a sip, letting the liquor burn down his throat, settling him.

"You're here. You're safe. You're protected by the most powerful witch in the kingdom. Not to mention Edvard and his ghost friends," Ridge reassured him. "And let me tell you, those ghosts went after the creatures with everything they had—we could *see* them. I don't want to get on Edvard's bad side," he added with a smile calculated to win a reaction from Rett.

Rett managed slow, steady breaths as the adrenaline spike waned. He knocked back the rest of the whiskey, gasping as it set his throat on fire, reminding him he was alive.

"I'm all right," he managed, under Ridge's skeptical gaze.

"Sure about that?"

Rett nodded. "It's just … I can't help thinking … that could have been me."

Ridge paled, shuddering. Rett guessed that the same awful thought had no doubt occurred to his partner.

"But it wasn't you," Ridge replied, keeping his voice firm and biting off each word. "We got you back. You fought hard to come home."

"How many more like that does Noxx have? Who were they—and why did he pick them?" Rett knew those questions would haunt him.

"After you and Kane dispatched the *kolvry*, Edvard was able to speak to their ghosts," Malachi said from the doorway, where neither Ridge nor Rett had heard him approach. "Even their spirits were ragged, but they remembered enough of themselves to tell him who they had been."

"And?" Ridge prompted.

"One was a servant who displeased Noxx. The other was a guard who was in the wrong place at the wrong time," Malachi replied. "The bodies were wounded badly enough that the possessing ghost was the only thing keeping the host alive. When the ghosts were forced out, the bodies died, and the hosts' spirits were freed. Edvard says they've moved on. I hope they have found peace."

"How many more like them do you think Noxx has made?" Rett's voice came out thin and strangled.

"No way to know," Malachi responded. "But we'll stop him, and then we'll do our best to find them and send them on."

Rett looked down, not trusting himself to speak.

"I also had a chat with the miller's ghost, thanks to that bracelet you took," Malachi said. "He's sure Noxx sent the men who killed him. He suspected they would find him eventually. Not because he knew so much about Noxx, but because he knew about a secret room where Letwick kept important documents. He told me how to find it at Letwick's mansion. You might want to check the next time you're nearby."

Ridge laid a hand on Rett's shoulder. "If you feel up to it, come out with us and eat dinner. And then you can fill us in on what happened after you passed out."

"You went to Green Knoll again?" Malachi asked.

Rett nodded and cleared his throat, but Malachi held up a hand to silence him. "Eat first, and let me give you something for the pain. You can tell us your story when you're ready."

He managed a grateful smile directed at Malachi and Ridge and then satisfied his pride by walking to the table without assistance. Kane gave him a nod of acknowledgment and stepped out of his way.

Ridge and Malachi kept the conversation light as they ate. Kane chimed in from time to time, but none of them seemed to expect Rett to keep up his end of the discussion.

Malachi brought out candied nuts and another bottle of whiskey with glasses for everyone when the dishes had been cleared away.

"I think something is wrong with Green Knoll," Rett said. "Brother Tom was worried about bad dreams and omens and tremors shaking the ground. I didn't say anything to him, but if there's magic involved in hiding the compound, could its power be failing?"

Malachi thought for a moment and then nodded. "That's certainly possible. The two most likely reasons would be that a witch is trying to break the spell that hides the monastery or that the witch who cast the original magic is growing weaker. Since there must be a reason you're drawn there, and someone thought it was important to protect the place, it's not a good thing that the energy is damaged."

"Tom and the other monks mind their own business. They don't bother anyone, and they never leave the compound. I don't want them to get hurt," Rett said.

"We'll do our best to protect them," Malachi said. "But first, we have to find them. Gil is tracking down any leads he can find, and Edvard is checking with the ghosts. We'll figure it out."

"Did you hear more from Gil about the regency council candidates?" Kane asked. "I have a bad feeling about that."

"Nothing of substance." Malachi sipped his drink. "But he's still digging. Gil believes that the Witch Lord is behind the selection process, advancing candidates he has a hold over or believes he can control. That would fit with Makary's pattern, picking people he can control as a power behind the throne."

"Sounds like what he'd do," Ridge agreed.

"Gil also says that the Shadows who stayed with the palace have been sniffing around the city, presumably looking for Ridge, since everyone thinks Rett is dead. Or maybe for Burke and Caralin," Malachi added. "I sent an owl ghost back to Gil with word of what happened. My suspicion is that the Witch Lord is working directly with Noxx."

"That never works out well for his collaborators," Kane observed.

"Not in the long run," Ridge agreed. "But they're usually too greedy to notice before it's too late."

"And I'm still searching for Runcian—King Renvar's witch—or his ghost, as well as Kristoph's ghost. I'm certain now that while someone else bound Kristoph's spirit, Runcian hid himself. Both workings took a lot of power to hide from me." Malachi smiled, confident and crafty. "But in the end, I'll find them."

"Enough serious talk for one night," Kane said. "Time for a game."

Malachi set out a jug of wine while Kane shuffled cards to deal. Rett begged off, managing an apologetic smile. "You always tell me not to push too hard," he said when Ridge looked at him as if trying to figure out what was wrong. "This is me, trying to listen. I'm going to go get some sleep."

Rett padded back to the room he shared with Rett, consciously keeping his shoulders square and head up like he wasn't practically asleep on his feet. Once he was out of sight of the others, he nearly stumbled and cast a quick, guilty glance over his shoulder, fearing the others might have heard his clumsy footsteps.

When he was inside their room and the door shut behind him, Rett sagged against it, nearly sliding to the floor as his knees threatened to buckle. His head throbbed, and his body ached from riding and fighting after his long convalescence.

Two visions in one day didn't help. They left him drained at the best of times, and recovering from the damage inflicted by Letwick's torturer meant Rett wasn't starting in good condition. But it was what he had to work with, and Rett would be damned before he let anyone down—especially Ridge.

Ever since Ridge, Kane, and Henri hauled Rett's barely functioning body and splintered mind from the fetid cell where his captors had broken him, Rett knew that the magic thrumming through his veins was different than before. How it had changed and what that meant, he didn't know, only that the shift felt permanent.

Even Malachi wasn't sure of the extent of the changes or how well Rett might be able to control his new abilities. Rett felt certain that if Ridge knew the degree to which his abilities had changed, he would have backed Rett into a corner and demanded answers, trying to assure himself that Rett was safe and sane.

Dreams plagued him every night. Sometimes they replayed jobs Ridge and Rett had done, only with a twisted ending that went terribly wrong. He had seen both of them die bloody more times than he could count. When it wasn't the two of them, it was Henri, Kane, Malachi, or other friends. Too often, he believed he was back with the duke and his torturer, that his escape had been a pain-fueled fantasy, and that Ridge and Henri were dead, so no one was coming to save him.

Rett woke panicked, drenched with sweat, heaving for breath. When he told Ridge they were bad dreams, he wasn't lying, but he hadn't come close to telling the whole truth.

Worse were the times when the magic flowed through him like fire, burning along every nerve. Like Ridge, Rett had only ever had the Sight—his ability to tell if a soul had been corrupted by dark powers—and occasional visions. Now, the visions came more often, in greater detail. Unlike the dreams, they were always true.

Despite his recent lessons with Malachi, Rett still didn't know how to control his heightened magic or how to keep it from drawing unwanted and dangerous attention. His abilities felt unstable, surging or waning unpredictably. Sofen hadn't tried to contact Rett directly by sending a vision, out of deference to his injuries. Rett appreciated that kindness and wondered whether he would be better able to receive a sending—and reply in kind, something he hadn't been able to do before.

While his body and mind had slowly mended, Rett knew he wasn't whole yet—and wondered if he might ever be. Malachi had healed the worst of his injuries and sped up healing on those he couldn't fix outright. Still, Rett knew his stamina hadn't fully returned. Joints and muscles still twinged, he was only gradually regaining his strength, and he hadn't even dared to see whether he could still aim his bow or matchlock.

I'm a liability, and we all know it—although the others are too polite to say so. I might eventually be fine, but Ridge needs me at my best right now. If I move too slow or collapse on a

*job, I could get us captured or killed. The kingdom doesn't
have time to wait for me to get better—not with the Witch
Lord still at large.*

He drew his knees up and rested his head on his arms,
choking back a sob. Rett had never felt so broken or hopeless.
His ability to rein in his emotions seemed as wrecked as the
rest of him, far from what being first a soldier and then an
elite assassin demanded.

I don't have any business out on a job until I'm not a danger to Ridge. He was right to team up with Kane.

As logical as it was for Kane and Ridge to hunt the Witch
Lord while Rett recovered, he couldn't ignore the jealousy
that stabbed through him at someone else taking his place
beside the man who had always been his best friend and his
brother of the heart, if not by blood.

*If I can't make a full recovery, I'll be damaged enough that
Ridge will have to leave me behind. Will Malachi let me stay if
I can be useful with magic?*

Rett was grateful to Kane and Malachi for their help, but
he still felt out of place in the tower. He missed the apartments he had shared with Ridge and Henri and the easy camaraderie. That had been his only real home—the three of them
together, thick as thieves.

"Rett?" Ridge's voice carried through the door. "I'm coming in."

Rett dragged his sleeve over his face and got to his feet,
crossing toward his bed in two strides before Ridge entered.

"I got worried," Ridge admitted. He held out a cup of hot
tea. "Malachi sent this—he said it will help."

Rett sighed. He was certain that he couldn't hide his breakdown, and so he sat on the side of his bed and cradled the cup
in his hands. "Thanks."

Ridge shut the door behind him and leaned against it. Rett didn't doubt that Ridge saw right through his pretenses. They had never been good at lying to one another. Not after so many years spent together.

"You did really well out there," Ridge said. "Held your own in the fight too. Not bad for the first time back in the saddle."

Rett shrugged, unwilling to trust his voice.

Ridge sat on the other bed, facing him, clearly undeterred even though Rett didn't meet his gaze.

"Getting hurt is part of this job," Ridge said, apparently determined to say his piece whether or not Rett wanted to listen. "Needing time to get better goes with that. We're the best damn Shadows in Landria because we do the job together. I need you to take the time to heal because saving the kingdom from the Witch Lord is going to require both of us—and our allies."

"There are things that need to be done. The danger doesn't stop just because I'm a wreck." Rett's voice was thick with emotion.

"You're not a wreck," Ridge defended in a sharp tone that drew Rett's attention. "You survived. You're sitting here talking to me, functioning. I know the ride and the fight took more out of you than usual, but that will get better."

"I don't want to be the reason you get hurt. Kane can keep you safer," Rett replied, even though the words tasted like ash. *It's not about what I want. It's about protecting Ridge and saving the kingdom.*

Ridge raked a hand through his hair, a move Rett knew meant he was trying not to show his frustration. "Kane is a good fighter. He makes a fine partner. But he's not you."

Rett looked up, searching for the lie in Ridge's expression and not finding it.

"You and I have fought together since the orphanage," Ridge continued. "I know your moves. Shit, I usually know what you're going to do before you do. That's why we're so good together. I trust you."

"Maybe you shouldn't … the way I am now."

Ridge glared at him. "Fuck that. You'll get back to how you were before—with a little extra."

"Did Malachi say that?"

Ridge nodded. "He doesn't want to push before you're ready, but he thinks that the drugged ointment Letwick used on you blew the doors off your magic. It's going to take time to figure it out."

"It's all a little terrifying," Rett admitted.

"So for the next little bit—just temporarily—Kane and I are going to follow up on some leads about Noxx while you and Malachi try to figure out just how much your abilities have changed and how to use them without hurting yourself." Ridge held up a hand to still the protest already rising in Rett's throat.

"*Temporarily*. While you heal. Just a little routine spying," Ridge assured him. "So that when we get to the important stuff, you're with me, like always."

"Spying is never 'routine.' Things can go wrong," Rett said, appreciating Ridge's efforts to reassure him even as he felt embarrassed about revealing his worries.

"I know. We'll be careful. After what the miller and his ghost said, I think there's a connection that we're missing that might make a difference. But we have to find Noxx or at least learn more about him."

"Promise me that you're not going up against him by yourself," Rett said. "You can't take on a witch without having some magic on your side."

"I won't unless there's no way to avoid it."

"Not exactly reassuring."

"You know that things don't always go as planned," Ridge said. "But that's where you and Malachi and Henri come in. Maybe the three of you can figure out how to find 'Brother Tom' and the monastery no one's ever heard of. I've got a gut feeling that monk has something to do with this. We're just missing too many of the pieces to know how it all goes together."

Rett chewed on the inside of his cheek as he listened. He knew Ridge was being truthful and sincere, and he recognized that his own insecurity and the way he'd been blaming himself made everything worse. Even knowing that, he found it difficult to pull himself out of the melancholy that had descended.

"All right. I've been wondering if I could find my way back to Brother Tom. When are you and Kane heading out?" Rett felt pleased that his voice sounded strong.

"Tomorrow. Kane knows some contacts who might be able to give us more information about Letwick's household and Noxx," Ridge replied. "I was trying to figure out how to tell you."

"The sooner we shut down the Witch Lord, the sooner our lives go back to what passes for normal for us," Rett said with a confidence he didn't feel.

"Thank you for trusting me," Ridge said, and Rett could see the heartfelt conviction in his eyes.

"Just don't die."

"You too."

Rett tamped down his feelings, hard, when he watched his best friend head out with Kane early the next morning. He knew that having Kane and Ridge investigating together was temporary. But he couldn't help feeling left behind, and Rett accepted that the emotions were part of his addled brain and the trauma of his captivity and torture.

Malachi laid a hand on Rett's shoulder. "Trust them to do what they do best."

Rett nodded and swallowed to clear the lump in his throat. "I do trust them, but that doesn't mean I don't worry."

"I understand." Malachi's tone let Rett know the mage meant it.

"We have work to do," Malachi said when he forced himself away from the tower's window. He turned to Henri. "We will need everything you acquired."

"I have it ready," Henri assured him, and he shot a cocky smile at Rett. "This is what I went to buy in Dorben's Crossing, if you wondered." He pulled a cloth bag from a bin in the tower's kitchen and began to lay the items out on the table.

"How does this work? Do I have to use that awful ointment again?" Rett asked, steeling himself for a reply he wasn't going to like.

The "flying ointment" was made from plant extracts known for their ability to provoke visions and psychic experiences. Used in small amounts, a skilled witch could control their mystical journey. Inflicted as a torture in large quantities, as had been done to Rett, it was like having his brain turned inside-out.

Malachi smiled and shook his head. "No. You don't have to use it. I will. We'll be linked, but that will buffer the worst of it for you."

Malachi brought candles and lit them, then combined the dried plants, tinctures, and powders that Henri had purchased along with ingredients from jars and vials in the cupboards. He used a piece of charcoal to mark sigils on the table's surface.

"Have a seat," Malachi said to Rett. Henri laid down a circle of salt and other protective powders around the table and two chairs, careful to remain on the outside.

"Henri is our backup," Malachi explained. "If this goes wrong, I've given him instructions on what to do and how to break us out of the trance."

Rett stared at him. "Trance?"

Malachi nodded. "I'm a necromancer, so my magic can grip your soul—leaving it unharmed and right in your body where it belongs," he hurried to add. "I'm going to connect us through magic and ritual and then use a mix of elements to let us 'drift' together. If you concentrate on finding Brother Tom, we may be able to find our way without putting you at further risk from the mixtures."

"What about you?" Rett didn't like the idea of Malachi accepting harm to protect him.

"I haven't been through your ordeal, so I have more strength to draw on. And the concoction I made was designed for a witch who planned to live through the event. Half of the damage Letwick and Doctor inflicted on you was malice, and the other half was ignorance," Malachi growled. "Either the duke didn't listen to his witch, or his mage is a dangerous pretender."

"They did all that to get me to tell them things I didn't actually know," Rett said quietly, unwilling to remember those awful days too clearly.

"I don't doubt that causing pain was a goal," Malachi said in a voice that promised vengeance for the harm done to

Rett. "Even so, they were amateurs, sloppy and stupid. The rules of magic try to prevent us from becoming like Yefim Makary."

Makary was the wandering mystic who had styled himself the Witch Lord and gathered discontented nobles and aristocrats to his cause. While he presented himself as a seeker of truth and a philosopher, his ramblings inevitably cast aspersions on the king and Landria's government, prompting two attempts on Kristoph's life before one succeeded and causing numerous attacks on his loyalists.

Behind Makary's homespun persona lay an educated, cunning mind and a thirst for power. Makary's chosen name hid his blood ties to the aristocratic Letwick family, a contender for succession.

Duke Letwick's execution at Ridge's hand removed that avenue for Makary to put a puppet king on the throne, but Makary had rebounded before from Ridge and Rett foiling his plans. Letwick had a younger brother, though no one had seen him in months—another threat to the crown Ridge and Rett would eventually need to resolve.

Rett had no doubt that the Witch Lord was busy reformulating his attack. To safeguard the throne from a new king controlled by Makary, they'd have to discover his strategy and outwit him.

"What do I need to do?" Rett might not be able to take on all the duties of his role as a Shadow just yet, but working this magic was something he could do that might make a difference. That made it worth the risk.

"Just take my hands when the time comes," Malachi said. "Physical contact is necessary so that my magic grips your soul, and you can 'ride along' with the potion's effects to take us elsewhere."

"Dream walking," Rett said, meeting Malachi's gaze. "When it happened to me the first time, I didn't know what was going on. Since then, it's been by accident because I was mostly dead. That's what you're making possible, without the dying part, right?"

Malachi nodded. "I won't say that any attempt to travel is exactly 'safe,' but there are definitely worse ways to go about it—as you discovered. We're going to avoid those."

"Ridge will storm the underworld to haul us back if this goes wrong," Rett warned.

"I'm well aware." Malachi didn't look like he was kidding. "Let's get started."

Henri hung well back from the salt circle, arms folded across his chest, expression grave. He had an array of items laid out beside him that Rett didn't recognize, but he felt sure Henri had over-prepared for his role. There was no one other than Ridge that Rett would trust more to save his ass if this didn't go right.

"Lead the way," Rett said.

Malachi drank some of the liquid and then dipped his fingers into the elixir and flicked it at Rett, making sure to add a few drops to each candle, careful not to quench the flames. The drops barely touched Rett, but he felt the effect of the potion through his link to Malachi. The necromancer took hold of Rett's hands, and the surge of power made Rett jolt as if he'd been struck by lightning.

Malachi didn't react. His eyes fluttered shut, and his head tilted back with an expression of concentration. The firm grip on both hands kept Rett anchored as he felt the magic flow through their connection.

Rett closed his eyes and focused on their link. Malachi's magic stirred deep in his core, and Rett felt something essential *loosen* inside him and float free.

He let himself drift in the current of Malachi's power. The tether of light that kept him linked to his body seemed gossamer thin. But it was more than he'd had before when his soul must have gone walkabout without a lifeline, carried on the currents and eddies of the flux and flow of creation's energies until it found a place called Green Knoll. That didn't exist.

Rett recognized the place immediately, something he tried to *think* at Malachi, whose presence he felt like a shadow at the back of his mind.

When Rett opened his eyes, he was inside the library in the monastery.

"We're here."

Or rather Rett was.

Rett realized the monastery had to be larger than his initial impression, but it still had the feel of an intimate cloister.

"Find him," Malachi sent.

Rett moved through the familiar corridors, pushing aside thoughts about how this place could be possible. He didn't see anyone, something that might have struck him as strange before if he'd had his wits about him. Brother Tom had mentioned other monks. Rett had only seen one other person—a stern monk who seemed to realize that Rett didn't belong.

The library felt *real*—solid to the touch, with a logical floor plan. He wasn't walking through walls or having whole sections appear and disappear.

And yet, something was wrong. Rett couldn't put his finger on it, but for as normal as the monastery seemed, it wasn't quite *right.* Maybe when he got back to Rune Keep, Malachi would know how to distill that feeling into words.

He could sense Malachi's presence with him and knew that the necromancer's bond kept him connected to his body and the real world. For this "trip," Malachi was present in

Rett's mind, but not in a way Tom or the other monks would sense. He trusted Malachi to bring him back safely, and that anchored Rett in a way that hadn't been possible during his previous visits.

Rett forged on, paying careful attention to all the details of the building as he moved silently through the corridors. He thought he recognized where he was and remembered the way to the library. That was where he had encountered Brother Tom before, so Rett decided to return and see if his luck held.

Several times Rett thought he heard voices, but he plastered himself against the wall in an alcove and didn't emerge until the voices had passed. Much as he was curious about the rest of the cloister, he needed to find Tom and see what they could learn.

The library door opened at his touch, and Rett looked around, taking in the whole room and its voluminous collection for Malachi's benefit. It struck Rett that the library's vast holdings seemed disproportionate to the small outpost of a dozen or so monks. The library looked like it had on his previous visit. Shelves packed with books covered the walls from floor to ceiling, with long wooden tables down the middle and doorways opening into other similar rooms, stretching on out of sight.

Is it some kind of repository of grimoires? An arcane library full of dangerous books with a handful of trusted guardians?

Rett walked beside the bookshelves in the main room, glancing at random titles. Sorted by subject into sections, he saw books and manuscripts on medicine, history, art, and government.

He moved into the second room and found more floor-to-ceiling shelves packed full with leather-bound tomes and fragile scrolls. Still sorted by subject, Rett saw biographies of past kings, as well as books on gardening, beer making, and warfare. The library's varied collection intrigued Rett, and the would-be scholar in him wished he could stay and examine the books more closely.

"You're not supposed to be here."

Rett wheeled and found himself facing Brother Tom. "I can explain—"

"Brother Kendrick says you're a threat."

Rett held up his hands in a placating gesture. "Give me a moment to explain, and then I'll go."

Tom looked wary, but then he gave a grudging nod.

"Landria is in danger. There have been attacks on the king, and he has no heir. The people behind the attacks follow a crazy mystic who is up to no good. We're trying to protect the kingdom and the monarchy," Rett told him, doing his best to phrase the information so as not to give too much away.

He remembered that the cloister had almost no outside contact, and he didn't want to overwhelm Tom with new information.

"How do I know you're telling the truth?" Tom was scared, and Rett cursed whoever had filled the man's head full of fear.

"I'm not lying." Rett relaxed his stance and smiled, hoping to rekindle the rapport he had felt with the monk on his previous visits.

"The person trying to harm the king is a witch. I haven't been able to find any materials in the libraries I can access that could help us stop the witch and save the king," Rett said. "Then I remembered what a good collection you have here, and I needed to see if you have something I can use. Please, the kingdom is at stake."

The young monk seemed to be extremely naive, and Rett wondered if he had come to the cloister as a student—or even an orphan like Rett.

"What do you need?" Tom asked. He cast a glance over his shoulder. "I can help you figure out where the books are shelved, although if you take something and someone notices, there'll be trouble."

"If we find something useful, I can look at it here and memorize it so we don't get caught," Rett reassured, figuring that Tom had come to a silent decision. "Thank you. I truly appreciate it. This might save the kingdom."

Tom blushed, looking down and giving a shy smile. "That's a lot for just showing you how the books are grouped."

Tom led Rett through the warren of rooms. As they continued their tour with Tom explaining the system the monks used to make their library easier to search, Rett wondered why Tom had suddenly agreed to help when his greeting had been prickly.

"Are you paying attention?" Tom called to Rett, who walked a few steps behind them. "There's a lot to repeat if you drift off."

"I'm listening. It's just a lot to take in," Rett assured him.

"I'm surprised you can come and go," Tom said as he continued to show Rett around. "None of the rest of us ever leave the cloister."

"I think you've got the best of it," Rett replied and meant it. Whatever this haven actually was, it felt far removed from court politics, disloyal nobles, and the dangers of the real world.

"That's what the older monks tell me. I wouldn't know. I've never been outside the compound since I came here," Tom confessed. "I was a foundling, left on the doorstep of a different monastery as a newborn. We—the monks and I—moved here shortly afterward—so I'm told. All I had of my mother was the blanket she wrapped me in. I have no idea who my parents are."

"I was an orphan too," Rett told him. "I don't really remember my family. You're lucky to have found such a good home. But you've never wanted to leave, see the big world?"

Tom shrugged. "I wonder about it sometimes. But all these books are like windows, showing me anything I want to see," he added with a sweeping gesture to indicate the vast holdings of the monastery's library.

Rett did his best to make a mental note of the many books and manuscripts. Quite a few of the tomes were grimoires, even more than he had hoped.

There was a time when Landria didn't restrict magic to the priests and the army. Were these books elsewhere until magic was banned—and moved here to protect them while keeping them out of reach?

"You said someone is trying to hurt the king?" Tom sounded worried, to a degree that surprised Rett since the monarch and the court must seem so abstract to the sheltered monk, like something out of a storybook.

"There's a bad man using magic to bewitch people so that they'll follow him. He would like to hurt the king and put someone he can control on the throne."

The look of shock on Tom's face was genuine and guileless. "That's terrible."

"Other researchers and I are trying to figure out how to stop him," Rett said, hewing as close to the truth as he could. "I thought that consulting the old books here might help. There aren't copies of many of them elsewhere."

Tom gave a fond look to the nearest shelf of books and let his fingertips slide along their spines. "I've been told that we have many very rare books—sometimes the only copies. The older monks warned me that some of the books should only be studied with a mentor's supervision."

"Have you read any of those?" Rett wondered what, other than grimoires, might be considered so dangerous.

Tom shook his head. "No, although I'm curious. But not enough to risk getting turned into a frog," he added with a smile.

"Probably a good thing," Rett replied.

"Brother Kendrick was surprised to see you. He doesn't seem to like you. Told me to stay away if you came back."

That must be the grumpy-looking monk I saw in the corridor. Did he figure I was an outsider—or did he have any idea who I am and where I came from?

"I hope I didn't cause any trouble for you. You've been very kind," Rett said.

Tom chuckled. "He gave me a stern lecture, but no harm came from it." He looked around, checking to make sure they were still alone. "He's the monk I like least," Tom confided in a whisper.

Rett smiled. "I can see why."

He felt the glowing thread that connected his life force to Malachi, and back to his body. Rett knew that he would need to return soon, but he hated to leave without solving the mystery of Brother Tom.

"Are you going to vanish again?" Tom asked. "I thought you might have been a ghost until Brother Kendrick took me to task about talking to you."

"I'll have to go, but I'll be back again. I'd like time to study the books. And I enjoy talking with you," Rett replied.

Tom sighed. "This is probably where I should tell you what Kendrick told me to say, about not coming back. But I like talking with you, and Kendrick is an old prune. The other monks are nice enough, and we talk about books we've read, research projects, what's going on with the farm and the animals and the brewery. But there's never any *news.*"

"That might not be a bad thing," Rett told him. "Most of the news isn't good."

"No, but it's 'new,'" Tom said. "I'm going to go for supper. No one should disturb you for at least a candlemark while we eat. That should give you time to get some research done. Safe travels—and come back soon!"

Rett ventured to find a shelf they had passed earlier filled with spell books. He knew he wouldn't be able to stay much longer, but he thought that he could share some of the most promising books through his link with Malachi to revisit if he was able to return.

He could tell the magic had started to take a toll. His head ached and he felt feverish. The golden thread tugged on him, warning that it was time to go.

Rett put the last book back on the shelf and swayed on his feet. He caught himself with one outstretched arm, knowing his visit was about to come to an end.

"Why are you back again?" The grumpy older monk came around the corner, glaring at Rett. "You are compromising everything by being here. You put our entire existence at risk. Go!"

Rett felt a psychic push just as Malachi jerked the energy that leashed between them, and the combination sent him reeling. The library vanished. Instead of the tranquil waves that bore him away at the beginning of the astral projection, Rett felt buffeted on a stormy sea, clinging to the golden thread to avoid getting swept away.

He fought down panic, afraid he might be lost forever on the wild currents or that the thread might snap and he would be adrift, unable to find his way back.

Why did Kendrick react like I was an enemy? Who does he fear?

Abruptly Rett was back in his chair at Rune Keep, gripping Malachi's hands hard enough to bruise, staring wide-eyed at the mage.

"Are you all right?" Malachi looked him over, worried.

Rett cleared his throat and tried not to fall out of his seat as vertigo threatened to make him lose his lunch. "I think so. Did you see everything?"

Malachi rose to pour a glass of water for Rett and waited until Rett drank it all before replying. "Yes, I saw what you saw." He refilled the glass and set it near Rett before sitting again.

"What did you make of it? What do you think of Tom?"

Malachi sat back and crossed his arms with a thoughtful expression. "I think that he and the monastery are real. But I suspect that they exist somewhere that has been profoundly altered."

"Altered—how?" Rett sipped his water and struggled against the oddest sense of not being entirely solid, as if his essence hadn't completely settled back into his body. "Like ghosts?"

Were we temporarily dead, and I didn't notice?

Malachi shook his head. "Not exactly. We were still alive—and so was Tom. But in the sense that ghosts sometimes exist in the same space as living people and sometimes don't ... maybe."

"I don't understand."

Malachi chuckled. "I'm not entirely sure I do either, yet. It's possible to bespell a place like a castle—or a monastery—and deflect people's awareness of it. The castle doesn't become invisible, but people walk by it without noticing or remembering.

Obviously, the bigger the building, the harder it is to hide. But that's not exactly what was going on. I don't think we were somewhere hidden—I think Green Knoll has been placed somewhere *outside.*"

Rett knew his confusion showed on his face. "Outside what?"

Malachi looked off for a moment as he thought, probably trying to figure out how to explain. "When you 'traveled' to the monastery, your essence got from here to there, but you didn't travel on regular roads. The way you went was outside what's normal."

"All right," Rett said, trying to understand.

"There are some places where the natural energies are potent. Folks tell stories about people disappearing or being taken by mythical creatures. Sometimes that's the case. But other times, it has to do with the energy of the place itself that opens up a doorway to somewhere in-between."

"Between?" Rett felt like he was being slow to comprehend, but his brain hurt just trying to wrap itself around what Malachi suggested.

"Imagine that you have a cupboard in your wall. It has a door on one side of the wall and a door on the other side. An object inside the cupboard could be seen from rooms on both sides of the wall, but it wouldn't actually be in either room," Malachi replied.

"I can picture that." Rett's head spun at the implications, but for now, he tried to just focus on the words and not think beyond that.

"Doing the same kind of thing to a location requires powerful magic, or a naturally occurring place-energy—or both. It isn't easy to create or sustain. But there have been stories about rips that open to the Between Places. Occasionally, they involve buildings that appear and disappear. A whole monastery with grounds—that would be quite an undertaking."

"And yet no one's heard of Green Knoll," Rett said. "Either as an existing monastery or as one from the past. Tom says they never leave. I haven't exactly walked in through the front door, so me being able to go there doesn't count for 'regular' people. And they get no news of the outside world."

Malachi nodded. "That would all support the idea of being somewhere between. But why would anyone expend a massive amount of magic or energy to do that?"

"Maybe they were hiding the library and needed caretakers." Rett thought about the warren of rooms filled with books. "Think about all the books about magic. Landria hasn't always outlawed people with abilities. Perhaps when things changed, someone was able to gather and hide as much as they could, along with researchers and librarians."

Malachi's fingers tapped on the table as he thought. "Maybe. Tom was obviously the youngest of the group when they 'moved' to Green Knoll. Moved from where? I wish the others were more accessible to question, although from what you've seen of Brother Kendrick, I don't think that approaching them would be advisable."

"Probably not. And I don't want to get Tom into trouble." Rett pondered for a moment. "I wonder how I always end up in or near the library with Tom? I certainly didn't know him before this. I don't see how I could have a connection. But I always come back to him."

"If he was a foundling, there's no way to even trace a name," Malachi agreed. "I'm sure this will end up being important, even if we don't know it yet. But after what happened at the end, try to avoid going by yourself. I've never heard of someone who went dream walking getting lost, but it would be good not to put that to the test."

"I agree," Rett replied wholeheartedly. Malachi went to the kitchen and came back with a plate of cheese, sausage, bread, and olives, which he placed between them.

"Eat. It will help ground you. And you're still gaining strength."

Rett hated being reminded that he was still damaged, but he couldn't refute the truth. Hearing that from Malachi bothered him less than it did when Ridge suggested the same thing.

"Thanks. I just wish I could get back to how I was, so I could do my job." Rett picked at the olives.

"I always thought that Shadows were as much about brains as brawn," Malachi replied, placing some of the cheese and meat on a slice of bread and taking a bite.

"We're supposed to be."

"Then what you're doing now should count. I don't know what Brother Tom and the monastery mean yet, but I think you've found your way there several times for a reason. Helping me figure that out is just as valuable as wielding a sword or shooting your matchlock."

"If Ridge got hurt—or worse—and I wasn't with him, I'd never forgive myself. We're supposed to watch out for each other."

Malachi rested his elbows on the table and leaned forward, meeting Rett's gaze. "You and Ridge have abilities the other Shadows don't. Because of what you've endured, your magic is even stronger. That may be the edge that enables us to win against the Witch Lord. Kane is an excellent fighter. He can protect Ridge. But only you can help me figure out how all the magic works together and what it means."

Rett took a deep breath, let it out in a sigh, and nodded. "I hope you're right. I'm just not sure where to go from here."

Before Malachi could answer, Rett heard the cawing of a crow. He looked up to see a large bird perched next to the glass of the narrow tower window. Rett frowned because instead of the coal-black of a normal crow, this bird was dark gray. When he stared at it, the image stuttered, and he realized what he was seeing.

"It's a ghost," Rett said, surprised and confused.

Malachi laughed. "It's from Gil. Odd humor between a medium and a necromancer."

"Is it a messenger—like Edvard?" Rett couldn't help being curious.

"Yes—which means Gil has news for us."

Rett had met Gillis Arends briefly before they fled for the tower. Gil was a medium who also had visions and was something of a renegade psychic righter-of-wrongs. As the youngest son of a nobleman, Gil had plenty of money and free time, as well as privilege and protection. He cultivated a wastrel reputation, then used his abilities to punish other high-borns for crimes for which their titles and connections would have shielded them from consequences.

He was too successful, and complaints reached King Kristoph, who gave Gil the choice between being locked up on house arrest or being assigned a minder—Luc Marchand, a sheriff whom Kristoph wanted to rein in for being overzealous.

Malachi opened the window and stuck his hand through the bars, making contact with the ghost bird. He closed his eyes as if listening intently. After a few minutes, his expression changed to one of concentration, and seconds later, the spirit vanished.

"What's the news?" Rett asked when Malachi opened his eyes.

The necromancer returned to sit at the table. "Gil is positioned to hear things that the rest of us might not because he moves among the aristocracy. When Kristoph got wise to Gil annoying the nobles, he still thought Gil was cheating instead of using ghosts and clairvoyance to win more than his share of card games."

"Interesting."

"Ironic," Malachi replied. "So Gil gathers information, and Luc uses his connections as a sheriff to run down leads. They're rather scary together, far more capable of causing trouble together than they ever were apart."

"Do you think Kristoph intended that?" Rett couldn't help asking.

"I've often wondered that myself. I don't know whether they ever would have found each other without the king playing unintentional matchmaker, but they're formidable as a team."

"The message must have been important for Gil to send a messenger."

Malachi grimaced. "It's his odd sense of humor. Regular people use carrier pigeons. Gil uses ghostly animals. I've been visited by cats, bats, rats, owls, even a vulture. I'm sure he finds it funny."

Rett suspected that beneath Malachi's protests, he was also amused.

"And?"

Malachi leaned back. "Confirmation of what we suspected or heard whispered. Gil says that since there's no heir, Duke Letwick is dead, and his brother has vanished, the Council of

Nobles is moving ahead to create a regency council to rule in the stead of a successor until a suitable heir can be found. Makary himself hasn't been seen in the palace city—he's still pretending to be dead—but Gil also confirmed that the Witch Lord has agents among the nobles who would likely be named to the regency council. So he would still be the power behind the throne as he always intended."

"Shit.

"Makary doesn't miss a trick," Malachi replied with a tired sigh. "And frankly, damn Kristoph for not leaving an heir. Yes, he was devastated when his wife and child died. I've been living with the punishment for that—although it wasn't my doing—for years. But he had an obligation to the kingdom not to leave it vulnerable to this kind of political scheming. And in that, Kristoph let his emotions get in the way of his duty, making it worse for everyone."

"Anything else?" Rett asked.

"Other than a couple of vulgar jokes he couldn't help passing along? Nothing of importance. Gil is keeping an eye on the potential regency council members. Luc says that everyone still thinks you and Henri are dead and that Ridge either died or fled the kingdom—which is good. Means they aren't looking too hard for you."

"What can I do to help? If we need me to go back to Green Knoll and search through the spell books, I'll do it. Please—I need to be useful," Rett said.

"I don't want you to risk traveling again to the monastery, at least until you've had time to finish healing. The books aren't going anywhere. You can't make unlimited trips there—it will drain you too badly and compromise your recovery."

"Then what?"

"I have a copy of some of the books you examined in their library. We can look at those and trust that the connections will eventually make themselves clear," Malachi replied.

"Then let's get started," Rett said, sounding more energetic than he felt. "Every moment lost is one we'll wish we had back in the final showdown."

CHAPTER FIVE

"I really wish the son of a bitch would stay in one place so we could kill him," Ridge grumbled as they rode.

Kane chuckled. "It's a pity that he inconveniences you when you're planning to murder him."

Ridge, Kane, and Henri were chasing down another lead on Noxx's whereabouts. Rett reluctantly remained at Rune Keep, working through old occult books with Malachi to find an explanation for what was happening to Green Knoll and how to stop it. Ridge couldn't keep from worrying about his partner, even though Rett and Malachi assured him that the damage from overexerting himself was healing quickly.

"Noxx might be hiding, but it hasn't prevented him from leaving a trail of bodies," Kane observed.

"Or creating his little *kolvry* army," Ridge added.

"Efficient—in an awful way," Kane said. "He snatches any crown loyalists he can find—or makes an example of people who fail him—and then breaks them, turning them into mindless killers. Then he sets them on better protected loyalists to get past their defenses or just cause bloodshed and chaos. No surprise that Noxx and the Witch Lord seem to get along."

"At least we know how to deal with the *kolvry*," Ridge replied. The matchlock's bullets worked on Noxx's tortured troops since, despite their appearance, they were nominally alive. Machetes and arrows would work as well, and Ridge considered it a kindness to put the twisted creatures out of their misery. While he had helped soothe Rett's nightmares about what might have been, Ridge couldn't stop his dreams from traveling in the same dark direction.

Since Rett wasn't with them to use his magic, Malachi had supplied them with potions that could taint the edge of a blade or the tip of a dart, pushing Noxx's magic out of reach and making it possible for them to capture the witch. They wanted Noxx alive—at least until Ridge could question him. After that, Ridge felt no hesitation about killing the dark witch even if he lacked an official, signed writ of execution.

"Is Noxx running from us or carrying out an agenda? And is he working on his own or for the Witch Lord?" Henri asked, bringing up the rear as they rode.

"Both, I imagine," Kane replied. "He certainly knows we're after him. If he is working with the Witch Lord, he can follow Makary's orders and eliminate potential enemies as long as he steers clear of us."

"And the Witch Lord's agenda?" Ridge asked, although he had a good idea of possibilities.

"Killing off anyone who gets in his way, however he can," Kane replied. "Takes care of the bold ones and intimidates the rest. Makes them less likely to fight for a place on the Regency Council. If Makary can put enough of his people in place on the council, he might not care whether they choose a king. He'll have the power he always wanted."

"And the means to break any support remaining within the palace for a legitimate successor," Henri observed. He glanced from Ridge to Kane. "I know how these things work. Never overlook the importance of the retainers. They're the ones who keep things running and know how everything gets done. They also protect—keep people from stealing the good silver and so on. If Makary puts his people in place, they could loot the treasury and make off with the paintings before anyone was the wiser."

Ridge sighed. *I don't know how we're supposed to stop the Witch Lord from getting his way now that Kristoph is dead. It's all too big, and we're too far away.*

"We've always suspected that Makary isn't a very powerful witch, despite the name he gave himself," Kane said. "Eliminating Noxx might do a lot of damage to Makary's plans," he added with a predatory smile.

This time, the tip about Noxx led them to a deserted mining town. Iron mines had built the village, but when the metal eventually grew too difficult to extract, the shafts were bricked up and abandoned and the miners left to find work elsewhere.

"What do you make of it?" Ridge asked as they paused on the outskirts of the town. Time and the elements had not been kind to the wooden structures. A tavern and a few shops stood empty on the main road, roofs damaged from long-ago storms. The handful of houses hadn't fared much better. In the distance, where the land rose on the far side of the village, Ridge saw what had probably been the mine office near where the shafts had been.

"Great place for a trap," Kane said.

"Those old mines could hide a lot of bodies," Henri noted.

"Can I say again that you have the most bloodthirsty valet I've ever met?" Kane asked with a laugh.

"He fits right in." Ridge shot a grin at Henri. He paused. "Noxx—and his *kolvry*—could be anywhere."

"From what we heard at the pub, the farmers steer clear of the old town," Kane reminded them. "They said people who come here don't leave."

"That's not at all unsettling," Ridge muttered. He couldn't shake his uneasiness, and experience had taught him to pay attention to his intuition.

They took the horses to a stream to drink, then tied them in a grove at the edge of town where they would have shade and grass and be screened from passersby. As they headed into town on foot, each of the men had weapons at the ready, on alert for any sound or movement.

"Someone's been here on horseback—recently enough that the hoof prints are still sharp in the dust." Kane pointed out.

Henri had already moved ahead, tracking the prints. "Over here." He beckoned for them to follow him to a ramshackle barn.

Kane and Ridge stood to the side while Henri swung the large door open. Inside were two horses, far too well-bred and groomed to be from any nearby farm. One look at the saddles, and Ridge got a sick feeling in the pit of his stomach.

"Those look like the horses Burke and Caralin had at the mill," he told the others. "Either they're already here, probably looking for Noxx or someone he's kidnapped, or he's got them, and we need to fix that."

"He won't have had them long," Kane replied. "If he can't grab you and Rett, they'd be a logical target. No matter how they might feel about you two, they're obviously not friends of the Witch Lord."

"I wouldn't be surprised to find out that Burke and Caralin are on Noxx's trail. But was he who they expected to find here, or did he bait a trap and lure them with something else?" Ridge wondered aloud.

"Let's find them first and ask questions later." Kane had a grim set to his jaw that told Ridge the spy expected trouble.

Ridge handed off the matchlock to Henri. The valet wasn't quite the sniper Ridge and Rett were, but he was by far the best shot Ridge had met aside from Rett.

"Find high ground," he told Henri. "Do that bird whistle thing if you need to warn us. If you see Noxx, shoot to kill. As much as I'd like to question him, we can't afford him to be wounded and still able to work magic."

"Got it," Henri replied as if the order was no different from sending him for supplies. He headed off, likely looking for a roof sturdy enough to support him.

Kane watched him go. "I don't know where you found him, but he's one of a kind."

"Don't go getting any ideas about tempting him away," Ridge joked. "We saw him first."

Although Ridge's intuition told him that the office and the mines were the place to go, they had to sweep every building on the way to avoid being ambushed. The wooden floors creaked beneath their weight while dust-laden cobwebs hung from the rafters and the ceiling lanterns, hinting no one had been through here in a long while.

"For a small mining town, it wasn't without some comforts," Ridge observed after they had cleared the shops and pub.

"People have to eat and drink. The mine owners probably made back everything they paid in wages," Kane replied.

Only three houses remained wholly intact. A dozen more lay in ruins or had only a foundation standing. "It looks like they just packed up and left—or maybe they didn't even pack," Ridge said.

Kane shrugged. "They probably didn't have much to take with them. Once the mines ran out, there was nothing left here to keep anyone. Without mining, the town didn't have a reason to exist. It's not on a trade route. The land isn't good for farming. Why would they stay?"

"I'm not the right person to ask about that," Ridge replied. "Staying in one place isn't something I have much experience with."

Ridge didn't know much about Kane's history, why he became a spy, or how he connected with Burke or Malachi. He couldn't help being curious, but he figured that if Kane wanted to share, he'd do it in his own time. *Not that it's really any of my business.*

Once they checked the last of the homes, Ridge signaled to Henri—wherever he was—that they were moving on to the office and mines.

"Can you see him?" Kane narrowed his eyes and raised a hand to shade them from the sun.

"No. But I know he's there. He's remarkably stealthy."

Ridge's nerves wound tighter the farther into the village they went. Every building they eliminated narrowed the remaining places where Burke and Caralin might be, as well as Noxx—and the *kolvry.*

I wish Rett were here. He might be able to sense whether Noxx is here. Kane is good. Rett is just as good—and I know his moves better. I don't want to get used to fighting with Kane. I want my partner back.

Ridge knew his reaction wasn't logical. Kane was a fine fighter and a clever spy. He was fortunate to have such a good substitute, someone he could trust to have his back. *And Rett will recover. He's stubborn. I just have to be patient.*

None of that mattered, not when they had a rogue witch to fight and possibly hostages to save.

Ridge wondered where Henri would find a vantage point. A glance flickered between him and Kane. *Time to go.*

The mine office remained in the best condition of the town's structures, probably because it was a single story made of stone and mortar. Squat and functional, it had outlived its makers and the mine itself.

Kane and Ridge had long blades in hand. Kane also had his bow, which let him provide backup from a distance. That gave Ridge the job of kicking down the door and getting out of the way to let arrows fly.

The rotten wood splintered from the force of his kick, and Ridge dropped, giving Kane a clear shot. He rolled and came up to a crouch, gripping his knife and ready to strike.

Nothing rushed forward from the dark interior, and no magic blast greeted their entrance. Ridge heard muted grunts, and as his eyes adjusted to the gloom, he saw two forms lying on the floor.

"I found them!" he called back to Kane. "Cover me!"

Ridge edged forward, wary of the shadows, expecting an attack at any moment. When nothing came at him, he let out a breath he hadn't realized he was holding and made his way toward the two bound bodies in the center of the room.

Burke and Caralin were tied hand and foot, gagged, blindfolded—and homicidally angry.

"It's me, Ridge," he told them in a low voice. "I'm going to cut the ropes. Don't hit me."

His blade made short work of their bonds. Caralin and Burke sat up, gingerly rubbing feeling back into their hands and feet.

"How did you know we were here?" Burke asked.

Ridge shrugged. "We didn't. It's your lucky day. We got a tip about Noxx. You two were a bonus."

"We?" Caralin asked.

"We have some allies working on research," Ridge told her. "Henri's here plus another friend."

"Kane," Burke replied.

"At your service," Kane replied from the doorway. "Not really. That was just to be polite. We need to get out of here before everything turns to shit."

The piercing whistle of a bird call ended abruptly with the unmistakable crack of a matchlock shot.

"Time to leave the party," Ridge said, waiting just long enough to make sure Burke and Caralin could stand. He and Kane both carried several extra knives and shared with the two Shadows.

Ridge felt an odd prickle run across his skin. *Magic? Is Noxx on his way back, or is he summoning his drugged killers to finish us all off?*

Another shot sounded from outside. The matchlock was good for eliminating enemies at a distance, but it wasn't fast to reload. That limited how effective it could be against a horde.

"Sounds like we've got company," Kane observed.

"We've got no idea how many of those *things* could be down in the mines," Ridge warned.

"You mean the feral corpses?" Caralin glanced from Kane to Ridge.

"That's as good a name as any—although they're not dead. Yet," Ridge replied.

Ridge thought about making the creatures come after them inside the mine office, where the doorway would force them to enter one or two at a time, making them easier to kill. That would have worked—if the windows hadn't been broken, giving the monsters more ways to enter.

"We're coming out!" Ridge shouted for Henri's benefit before he and Kane barreled outside one after the other, quickly followed by Burke and Caralin.

More than a dozen *kolvry* gathered between the mine office and the rest of the abandoned town. Henri shot and scored again, dropping one of the creatures in its tracks, but the beings weren't likely to hold off their attack to allow Henri to pick them off.

Then, the monsters charged.

Ridge swung his machete, severing a head from its neck and soaking him in blood. *Warm—they're still alive, and they were people.*

Kane scaled the stone walls of the office to use the vantage point as an archer to reduce the numbers of their attackers, firing arrows faster than Henri could reload the matchlock. That left Ridge, Burke, and Caralin still badly outnumbered against a foe that seemed to feel no pain or fear and sought nothing but bloodshed.

Another *kolvry* hurtled toward Ridge, and he swung again, slashing the creature open from ribs to groin. Stinking, steaming entrails spilled from the cavity onto the ground, but the creature barely slowed before Ridge's second strike slashed through the neck.

Caralin and Burke had each put down two of the magic-made monsters. Ridge didn't have time to count the bodies Henri and Kane felled, but there were still too many on their feet and crowding closer.

"Watch out!" Caralin shouted, and Ridge turned as one of the *kolvry* grabbed for his sleeve, then yanked him in close—too close—to teeth.

Ridge went with the momentum and thrust his knife in and up before pushing away. Despite the blood pouring from its body, the *kolvry* didn't let go, holding on to Ridge's jacket with a rictus grip. With another one just a few steps away, Ridge brought his blade down hard on his attacker's wrist, severing the hand that remained clenched on his coat as he stepped up to meet the next threat head-on.

He lost track of how many he killed or how much time passed. The matchlock's report provided a deadly rhythm. When Kane ran out of arrows, he joined the others on the ground and waded into the fray. Ridge's world narrowed to the opponent in front of him, trying to dodge a short sword wielded with disturbing skill.

This new opponent wouldn't quit, despite wounds that would have stopped a battle-hardened warrior. It was fast enough to dodge blows that would have ended the fight quickly, and it ignored pain even though one arm hung useless, blood poured from a deep belly wound, and a slice across the chest flayed skin from the white ribs beneath.

The *kolvry* lunged for Ridge. Ridge sank his blade between the battered creature's ribs, into its heart, and watched what life remained stutter and then go dark as the monster sank to the ground, mercifully dead.

"Is that all of them?" Kane asked as they looked around the open space that had become a killing field. They were all drenched in blood, looking like revenants themselves.

Ridge and the others remained on alert, tense and ready to strike, but no new attackers emerged from the mines. After a few minutes, they dared to lower their weapons and looked at each other, still jittery with the adrenalin of the fight.

"I thought I saw someone I recognized." Caralin kept her long knife in hand as she strode past the bodies until she stopped, looking down with an expression of grief and revulsion. Ridge joined her a moment later; he didn't know the dead man.

"His name was Vann," she said quietly. "One of the last new Shadows before Kristoph died. Barely out of training when it all fell apart. Heard he went missing. Guess we know what happened."

Ridge and Rett had kept their distance from most of the other Shadows, necessary since many of the other elite assassins disliked them for their unconventional methods, a penchant for breaking rules, and their peerless kill rate. It didn't help that neither of them came from titled or wealthy families, unlike many who rose to prominence in the army. Ridge and Rett had risen on skill alone.

"We need to get out of here before Noxx realizes his creatures didn't finish the job," Kane warned.

"We can't just leave the bodies for the scavengers," Caralin protested.

Kane crossed his arms over his chest. "Why not?"

Henri's ear-splitting whistle turned every head his way. He pointed toward the nearest tumbledown house. "These old buildings should catch like tinder. How 'bout we drag them inside and burn it down on top of them?"

Ridge couldn't help smiling at the valet's no-nonsense solution. Henri stood guard with the matchlock as Ridge and the others dragged the bodies and severed parts to the nearest house, tossing them inside in a heap. They pulled down loose boards from other ruins to stack around the corpses, then Kane doused the bodies with whiskey from a jug in his saddlebags and sparked flint and steel to set the fire. The flames caught quickly in the dry wood.

"We can't leave looking like this," Burke said, gesturing to their blood-soaked clothing.

"Noxx could be back at any moment," Kane argued with his former boss. "We've stayed too long already."

"Noxx be damned—we'll be set upon by every guard in the kingdom if we turn up looking like brigands covered in blood," Caralin warned.

"I saw a well on the way in," Henri said. "If it hasn't gone dry, we should be able to pull up enough water to rinse away the worst."

They followed Henri back to the area near the pub, then used the bucket and rope Kane brought with them to haul up enough frigid water to fill the trough behind the inn. That made it easier to sluice off the rapidly drying blood and gory gobbets.

"How long since you were captured?" Ridge asked Burke as they scrubbed away the gore.

"Yesterday—I think. Had a tip that there were 'magic monsters' roaming the area and figured the Witch Lord might have a hand in it. They got the jump on us, and no matter how many we killed, more kept coming." Burke sounded chagrined at their failure.

"Those creatures tied you up?" Ridge hadn't thought any of the *kolvry* looked coherent enough to pull off a kidnapping.

Burke shrugged. "We both went down fighting, hit hard enough to pass out. When we woke, we were like you found us. I've no idea why they didn't kill us." He looked at Ridge. "You weren't looking for us. Why are you here?"

Ridge wasn't going to admit that they'd gotten the tip from Gil. "Still chasing Letwick's witch, Noxx. He was here long enough to capture you and make his monsters, but he's gone now."

"We can't know for sure that he's the one who captured us," Burke protested.

"No, but he's the most likely suspect, considering those sorry bastards we killed are his handiwork," Ridge replied. He wiped the worst from his stained coat and turned it inside out, figuring that from a distance, that would be noticed less than the blood.

"Where's Rett?" Burke gave Ridge an appraising look that, as usual, probably told him more than Ridge wanted to reveal.

"Recovering. He got banged up pretty bad in another fight with these things, so he sat this one out." It was mostly the truth, Ridge figured, even if it left out most of the important details.

"The word I hear from the city isn't good," Burke told him as they dried off the best they could, shuddering at the ice-cold well water. "Without an heir or a clear succession, the government eventually grinds to a halt. The seneschal and exchequer and their staff can only do so much on their own. The nobles who are left from Kristoph's advisors have been threatened by the Witch Lord and his followers, so they're playing it safe. Makary's supporters are pushing out the loyal palace staff and replacing them with their own people."

"What do they want?" Ridge asked, aghast that so much could go wrong so quickly.

Burke shrugged. "What thieves always want—for the gate-keepers to be gone and the guards to look the other way. They want to grant favors to their friends, who will repay them in kind, or bend the law to their advantage, or punish rivals. Nothing for the good of the kingdom; everything to line their own pockets."

Ridge pushed down the anger and sorrow he felt, needing to keep a clear head. "And what of the rest of the kingdom? Have you heard anything? Out here in the countryside, news is scarce."

Ridge and Burke stepped back from the trough to allow Kane and Caralin to wash. Only Henri managed to avoid being splattered by the carnage.

"Without the palace in order, services are breaking down throughout the kingdom," Burke said with a heavy sigh. "If the guards don't get paid, they don't patrol—unless a noble recruits them for his private force. Ships in the harbor have problems unloading their cargo because the Customs House isn't open regular hours. Taxes aren't being collected, so government workers aren't being paid. It's bad—and it's getting worse."

Ridge hadn't given much thought to how the kingdom functioned. Now, he realized that he had been able to take the services for granted because they worked seamlessly without attracting attention.

"Can the Witch Lord break things so badly that it can't be fixed, even if a suitable heir was found?" It rattled Ridge to think of Landria being fragile enough to fall apart, but he knew such a fate had befallen other kingdoms.

"It depends." Burke sounded more resigned than Ridge had ever heard. "On how long it goes on. Without services from the palace, the nobles will raise armies for protection. Rival factions will vie for control of trade at the harbor and borders. Instead of a unified kingdom, we'll have warlords fighting over territory, like it was before Kristoph's grandfather and father brought them to heel. And if the regency council members are Makary's corrupt friends, it will be worse."

"We need to go," Kane warned again once they looked halfway presentable. "After that fight, we're not in any shape to beat Noxx if he comes back. I hate to say it, but we need to fall back. We need to be at our best to have a chance of beating him—and we're not right now."

"Thank you," Burke said, and Ridge looked up at the unexpected acknowledgment. "I didn't think Caralin and I would get out of that one."

Ridge played it off like it didn't matter. "We couldn't exactly leave you there," he replied. "And you saved our asses with the *kolvry*, so I'd say we're even."

"I'm sure we'll cross paths again," Caralin said. "Try not to get killed until we can save Landria."

Ridge snorted at the backhanded expression of concern. "Yeah. I'll definitely give it my best shot. You too."

"Are we *done yet?*" Kane snapped, not even trying to hide his frustration.

Ridge nodded and managed a cocky grin. "Yeah. We're done. For now. Let's go."

When they returned to Rune Keep, Kane got them into the lowest level of the tower and stopped Ridge and Henri before they could climb the stairs. "There's a place to clean up on this level. I can draw water from the cistern, and we keep extra clothing here for situations like this." Kane smirked. "Malachi hates it when the living quarters smells of blood."

It took harsh soap and several rinses, but by the time they went upstairs, they had washed the stink of battle from their skin and hair. The borrowed clothing hung loosely on Henri, who had to roll up the trousers, and Ridge's were a bit short and small, but it felt good to be clean.

Rett and Malachi looked up as they entered, both immediately giving them a head-to-toe once-over, searching for injuries.

"Are you hurt?" Rett asked. When he did not get an answer, he added: "There's warm food on the hearth and bowls next to it. Have as much as you want—we made a lot."

The main floor smelled of venison, leeks, and potatoes, and a plate of cheese and dried meat sat out on the table, along with toasted bread. A jug of ale and a flagon of wine were beside several glasses, and a pot of tea warmed on the hearth.

Ridge finally felt the events of the day hit him, and he made a plate, then sagged into a chair. "Talk to us while we eat. I'm not ready to explain what happened."

"Gil sent a report with a ghost vulture," Malachi replied, rolling his eyes at the over-the-top messenger. "He's gotten some insight into what drove King Renvar and more about Runcian, his witch."

"Tell us," Kane said, digging into his food. Henri pulled up a chair and did the same.

"King Renvar's father united Landria into the kingdom as it is now," Malachi replied. "Prior to that, warlords and powerful merchants had carved out fiefdoms with private armies. Renvar's father was, by all accounts, an excellent warrior and a skilled general. Ruthless, cunning—and not shy about relying on witches to help him with his conquests.

"He raised Renvar in the same fashion, a warrior-king. But by the time Renvar came to the throne, most of the hard work of uniting the kingdom was finished and that left mopping up and establishing the central government. Fortunately, Renvar understood what needed to be done and surrounded himself with competent administrators."

Malachi paused to take a sip of whiskey. Ridge wondered how much effect alcohol had on the mage.

"Renvar never forgave the noble families that were the hardest to bring into the kingdom. He couldn't afford to just kill them, but they were a persistent problem with minor insurrections popping up from time to time and subtle betrayals.

The Letwicks were the worst of them—not the least because a Letwick had been the other strong choice for the crown. He always suspected them of trying to find a way to undermine him," Malachi added.

"And he would have been right," Rett said, setting down his glass.

"So it appears," Malachi agreed.

"When did the kings stop liking witches?" Henri asked, having finished his food in record time. "And why? I always thought magic came in handy."

"According to Gil, Renvar and his chief mage, Runcian, worked together successfully for many years. Runcian helped the king achieve his military victories and protected him against his enemies. But that all came crashing down at some point, and Runcian disappeared."

Ridge quirked an eyebrow. "Did the king have him killed? I'd think that might prove difficult if Runcian was as strong a witch as you're suggesting."

"Gil's still looking into what happened, but it seems more likely that after the dispute, Runcian escaped the king's ire and went into hiding, or traveled far enough beyond Renvar's reach to keep his freedom," Malachi replied.

"After Runcian, Renvar never retained witches of similar power and became far more suspicious of anyone with strong magic. Kristoph would have been in his teens, and he must have picked up on his father's mistrust. He saw magic as a tool and recognized its value and danger, but he never trusted his witches, even those of us who were completely loyal." Malachi's sigh spoke volumes. He stared off for a moment and took another sip of his drink.

"Where could Runcian have gone that the king couldn't find him?" Ridge ran his finger over the rim of his glass.

"Out of the kingdom," Henri suggested. "If he got far enough from the border and kept his head down, he could find somewhere and settle down, and no one would be the wiser."

Rett looked thoughtful, then shook his head. "For some reason, that doesn't sound right to me. It's logical—and maybe the wisest course. But Runcian put a lot of his life into building Landria and fighting for it—and protecting Renvar. I doubt they'd fight over something minor. So whatever happened, maybe Runcian thought he was fighting *for* what was best for Landria, even if Renvar disagreed."

Malachi nodded. "Interesting. Is that a guess or some other *knowing*?"

Rett shrugged. "A guess, I think. But it makes sense to me. I don't think Runcian was a traitor or that he meant harm to the king. Maybe Renvar lost himself in the power of the crown and asked Runcian to do something that made him balk. Perhaps even something that violated a moral code Runcian thought he had once shared with Renvar."

"Does Gil know anyone who might have known Runcian personally?" Ridge asked. "He's got a rather large network of contacts."

"The falling out between Runcian and Renvar was close to thirty years ago," Malachi replied. "I doubt many people were privy to the reasons—the real reasons, not what Renvar might have concocted after the fact to explain his witch's absence."

"Could Runcian still be alive?" Ridge asked.

"It's possible," Kane replied. "Although if he's stayed hidden this long, I doubt we'd find him unless he wants to be found. And frankly, with the mess the kingdom is in right now, I wouldn't blame him for deciding not to come back."

"He might be an ally against the Witch Lord," Rett suggested.

"Unless he went to the other side of the ocean, he already knows what's going on in Landria, and he hasn't stepped up. Maybe he feared Kristoph. But we've been fighting the Witch Lord for a while now, and Runcian couldn't be arsed to help. We're better off without him," Kane said, anger coloring his tone.

Malachi looked at his partner quietly for a moment, and Ridge guessed he understood the betrayal beneath the rage.

"I don't think he's still alive," Malachi said. "But I also haven't been able to reach his ghost. Unlike Kristoph, I doubt he's bound. He may have moved on or died in such a way that his spirit could not return."

Rett frowned. "What would it take for that to happen?"

Malachi sat back in his chair and gestured toward one of the bookshelves full of old manuscripts. "There are many powerful spells that require the death—and soul—of the witch who does the working. I have a hunch that was Runcion's fate, although what sort of spell that involved, I wouldn't be able to guess."

"I still think we might find out something important if we can get a better look at the library at Green Knoll." Rett didn't flinch at the look Ridge shot his way.

Ridge hated how vulnerable and deathlike Rett appeared when he tranced or went soul-walking. Every time, he feared his friend might not come back and would wander forever. He knew Rett would argue that the possible gain was worth the risk, but Ridge never liked the thought of Rett going where he couldn't follow to watch his back.

"What happened to Letwick's family after his death?" Ridge asked.

"They went into hiding," Kane replied. "The main manor house is abandoned. Even the servants are gone. I think they feared that the charges of treason would cost them everything and they ran."

"The duke was alone at his hunting 'cabin.' How many homes did he have? If Noxx had a habit of imposing on Letwick's generosity, there'd be nothing to stop Noxx now that the duke is dead."

"You think Noxx might be hiding on the duke's lands?" Rett asked. "That could make him easier to find."

Kane and Malachi exchanged a look. "Not a bad theory," Kane said. "Did the miller's ghost happen to mention the duke's properties?"

"He talked about the manor and the hunting cabin," Malachi said. "Also a river house. I suspect he had an apartment in the city for when he needed to be at court, but it would be too dangerous even for Noxx to go there."

"Assuming the miller knew all of the places the duke owned," Kane mused. "There could be other family properties."

"But those wouldn't be deserted," Ridge pointed out. "The extended family doesn't have a reason to flee without a new king looking for vengeance. It makes more sense for Noxx to go somewhere no one will see him."

"I agree," Rett spoke up. "It's worth starting with the Letwick homes and seeing what we find."

"That doesn't mean it will be any easier to get to him," Kane warned. "He'll be on familiar territory. That gives him an advantage. And he won't be alone—he'll have *kolvry* to protect him. He's not going to quit without a fight."

"Let him fight," Ridge growled. "That will just make destroying him even more satisfying. He needs to pay for his hand in killing Kristoph—and what he did to Rett."

Rett looked away, and Ridge knew his partner remained troubled about the damage from Letwick's torture. That alone made Ridge more determined to punish Noxx. *He didn't just damage Rett's body. He took his confidence and hurt his mind.* To Ridge, that was even worse than Noxx's part in planning Kristoph's death.

"Noxx has to have figured out that we found Burke and Caralin," Kane said. "I doubt he'll risk going back to the mining town. So we'll have to start over looking for him—and have a better plan in place in case we find him."

"If we can find Noxx, maybe he'll lead us to the Witch Lord," Rett mused. "Gil thought they were working together. So Makary must have some way to contact Noxx. I doubt he'd risk himself to meet in person."

"Makary doesn't have much magic of his own, but if Noxx is helping him drain the life energy of the people he turns into *kolvry*, it could strengthen what Makary can already do," Malachi said.

"Seems to me that Noxx needs Makary more than the other way around," Henri observed.

"Makary has people on the inside at the palace. Noxx served a purpose with Kristoph's death, but now he knows too much. He might get ideas about trying to take advantage of Makary. That could undermine everything Makary's building with a regency council. If we're lucky, Makary might take care of Noxx for us."

That would be fitting, but Ridge had to admit feeling cheated of his vengeance.

Kane looked at Ridge as if guessing his thoughts. "Don't worry—I suspect you'll have a chance to get a shot at him before it's all over."

"Killing Noxx won't get me what I want," Ridge replied. "Not completely. It won't bring Kristoph back, or stop the Witch Lord, or un-do what Letwick did to Rett. But it would be satisfying to be the one who ends him."

CHAPTER SIX

The cloud of dust raised by three horses at full gallop threatened to choke Ridge, but he figured that was just one of the ways he might die in the next few minutes.

"They're gaining on us," Henri shouted as if Ridge hadn't known. Kane glanced over his shoulder, then crouched low and urged his horse for more speed.

How the fuck did the Witch Lord's henchmen recognize us? Ridge didn't have time to ponder that question. They couldn't ride at this pace for long, and Ridge hadn't come up with a brilliant plan to outwit the men chasing them.

If they're hired muscle with magic or who are good enough to ride and shoot a bow, we'll be dead before I can figure out how to escape.

The ruffians began their pursuit once Ridge and the others left the barren lands around Rune Keep, on roads that wound through small towns and farming villages. Even choosing the most remote roads to get to Letwick's properties, they couldn't completely avoid inhabited areas.

Since they had altered their appearances to avoid recognition, Ridge figured there had to be a spell of some kind, perhaps triggered when they crossed a boundary. However it worked, four armed riders, who weren't Shadows or in the livery of real guards, had shown up behind them, closing fast.

The market town wasn't far ahead. Ridge didn't fancy riding in at breakneck speed—hardly a way to remain unnoticed—but he also hoped the toughs chasing them would think twice about doing murder with an audience.

If we can get to the bridge on the other side of town, we'll have a better chance if it comes down to a fight. Letwick's lands aren't far beyond that.

The shoppers and farmers in the market square looked up at the sound of their horses. Ridge saw that they had attracted the notice of guards as well and wondered if there would be a fight over who got to kidnap them.

He chanced a look over his shoulder as they thundered toward the edge of town. Their pursuers suddenly veered off on a side road, but whether it was the sight of the guards or an unwillingness to transact their business in front of witnesses, He didn't know.

Ridge reined in his mount, slowing to a walk as they approached a curious crowd and three guards who looked far too interested. He was already scanning for an escape route.

The guards stepped out to block their path. "What's the hurry?" The captain glowered at them.

"We were being chased by brigands," Ridge replied, hoping this encounter didn't turn ugly.

"Brigands, huh? Where are they?"

"They veered off just before we got to town—must not have wanted to rob us with an audience," Ridge said.

The captain gave Ridge a hard look, and his eyes narrowed. "Hey, aren't you—"

Ridge pulled back hard on his reins, and his horse reared and kicked. The guards scattered to get out of the way, and with a cry, Ridge and the others galloped past.

By the time the angry guards regrouped, Ridge could see the bridge. He had no idea how they were going to shake the guards, and their horses were tiring fast.

"Get across, and leave the rest to me," Henri shouted.

They clattered across the bridge, horses foam-flecked and sweat-slick, and Ridge swore his heart was pounding as hard as his mount's. He hunched low, trying to gain any advantage for speed, bones jolting with every beat of the hooves.

When they reached the other side of the bridge, Henri's horse had barely stopped before the valet swung down to the ground, found something tied to a post at the end of the bridge, and struck a spark with flint and steel. A moment later, he was back in the saddle as their pursuers neared the other end of the bridge.

"Ride like demons are after you!" Henri yelled and took off once more as fast as his horse would carry him.

Ridge glanced over his shoulder to see the guards start across the bridge.

The explosion nearly made him lose control of his horse as the frightened animal shied and bucked. Even though they were a good distance away, bits of wood pelted him, hurled by the force of the blast.

Ridge wheeled his horse and squinted to see through the billowing cloud of dust.

Half the bridge was gone, and the guards were nowhere to be seen.

"Well, that was unexpected." Kane blinked away the rock dust and stared at the ruined bridge.

"I always say the simple solutions are the best," Henri said, brushing off his hands. "I rigged those barrels of gunpowder a couple of weeks ago when I went out for supplies. Had a feeling we might be paying a visit to Duke Letwick's property and figured we'd need a distraction either coming or going."

"A...distraction?" Kane echoed, looking a bit thunderstruck.

"By our standards, that was subdued," Ridge observed.

Kane looked from Ridge to Henri and then shook his head. "I thought assassins were supposed to be stealthy."

Ridge and Henri exchanged a grin. "Where's the fun in that?" Ridge replied, now that his heartbeat slowed from its frantic pounding. He flicked his reins, and the others fell in beside him.

"Where are we going?" Ridge asked Kane when they paused at a stream to water the horses. "You're the one who got a tip about Letwick's witch. Please tell me we're on the right side of the river."

Kane smirked. "It's a little late to worry about that now, don't you think? Letwick's estate should be a few miles west of here if my source is right. There's an old plague shrine on the land—hasn't been used since the last great fever swept through here."

"Plague shrine?" Ridge asked as a faint memory rose at the words.

"When a fever or a pox strikes, people don't want rites for the dead taking place in the same space where they go to leave their offerings for the gods or have blessings done," Henri explained. "They built shrines near burying grounds that were only used to send off the dead. Priests could say the final prayers and perform the passage rituals without putting anyone else at risk—except themselves."

Ridge frowned, chasing a ghost of a memory. "My family died in the last plague," he said after a few moments of silence. "I was very young. But I remember that priests came to take the bodies and said something about a shrine. I didn't understand why I couldn't stay with them."

"What makes you think Letwick's witch is here?" Henri asked.

"I've been poking around, looking for places Letwick owned," Kane said. "Noxx might prefer a smaller, more easily defended building to the main mansion. I'm still trying to figure out what he and the Witch Lord are up to, although I guess I'm not surprised they're working together."

"Not surprising in hindsight, now that we know Makary and Noxx are Letwick relations. Makary was already moving his game pieces into position and giving himself alternatives," Ridge mused. "He's a murdering son of a bitch, but unfortunately, he's also pretty damn smart."

"Intelligent criminals are the worst kind," Kane agreed. "I suspect Noxx was placed with Letwick as both a helper and a spy for the Witch Lord. He's sure to have been beholden to Makary."

"He came here because of his connection to Letwick?" Ridge asked, noting that after a few turns, the road they traveled looked overgrown and deserted.

"Noxx ran when we upended the duke's plans. Where else could he go but back to Letwick's lands? He was a frequent visitor to the manor house but didn't live there, and he probably couldn't go back to wherever he had been living because he knows we're after him, just like he didn't go back to the mining town," Kane replied. He'd gotten Gil's ghost birds to keep surveillance on the area, but Noxx never came back. "Letwick had a huge estate. And when I did enough poking around, I heard about the old plague shrine."

"Nice work," Ridge said. "You'd have made a good Shadow."

Kane snorted. "I don't take orders well, and I don't blow up nearly enough buildings to qualify."

"Burke would tell you that Rett and I aren't particularly good at the taking orders part either. And Henri blows up more things than we do."

"I learned from the best." Henri grinned.

"I wish Malachi could come with us," Ridge said. "I can't blame Rett for not wanting us to go up against Noxx without a witch of our own."

"Unless you've got one to spare, I don't see any witches helping us," Kane replied. "Rett needs Malachi more than we do at the moment. But I've trapped witches before by myself. It can be done—it's just damn dangerous."

"It would be a lot easier to use the matchlock to put a bullet in his head," Ridge muttered. "Simple. Direct. Final."

"Except that we need to interrogate him, or did you forget that part?" Kane countered.

"I didn't forget. I was just having a nice little revenge fantasy, that's all," Ridge said. "He might not have tortured Rett himself, but he supplied everything Letwick and his 'doctor' used to do it, including that damn flying ointment."

"When we're done with him, you can do the honors," Kane reminded Ridge. "I won't stand in your way. Noxx deserves it for what he did to Rett, and I doubt Rett was his first victim. But if he had a personal vendetta against the king, that means he wasn't acting merely out of loyalty to Makary. And I think that finding out his connection could be very important."

"Whether it is or isn't, we still get to kill him, right?" Henri clarified. "He's got it coming."

Kane turned to Ridge, only partially joking. "Is your valet always this bloodthirsty?"

Ridge shared a look with Henri over Kane's shoulder. "Usually, yes."

Kane shook his head. "Gods help us all," he muttered.

They secured their horses in a stand of trees far enough from the shrine to avoid notice.

Ridge fully acknowledged that their plan was insane. He'd end up begging Rett's forgiveness when they returned because even by their admittedly unconventional standards, the odds were not in their favor. Having their own witch would increase the chances of success astronomically, but true witches were scarce, and Malachi couldn't be spared.

Which meant they'd had to improvise.

Henri would provide the distraction and lure Noxx out of his shelter. Kane had darts with their tips coated by the potion that would make a witch groggy and temporarily dampen his magic. Once Noxx was down, Ridge would help restrain the witch after Kane gave him another dose of the potion.

That second dose, Malachi assured, would keep Noxx awake and able to answer questions while pushing his magic even farther beyond his reach. Malachi had told them Kristoph's witch-finders had used something similar on him when he'd been captured and forced into Rune Keep, so he could attest that the potion worked in practice as well as theory.

Ridge and the others came in sight of the shrine, a stone building next to an overgrown field filled with cairns and tombstones. Weeds choked the road leading up to the doorway, and ivy threatened to engulf the structure. The dark facade and windows devoid of ornamentation gave it a somber feel. Regular shrines were usually bedecked with waving flags, ringing bells, fireworks, and colored smoke heralding celebrations and feast days, a stark contrast.

Henri moved into the thick brush not far from the shrine's door. Ridge circled to enter from the rear once Kane made good his shot.

They gave Henri a few minutes to get set, and Kane gave the signal. From a thick stand of brush came a furious ringing of cowbells and the jangle of tambourines. Ridge knew Henri had hung the noisemakers from tree branches and worked them with ropes from a safe distance, but they still put up a godawful racket intended to force anyone inside the plague shrine to investigate.

Ridge took advantage of the noise to go around to the other side of the building, making sure Noxx didn't escape. At Kane's shout, Ridge broke down the back door and crossed through the open chapel area. A slender man lay in a heap at the front entrance. Ridge helped Kane drag Noxx back inside.

From his bag, Ridge grabbed a coil of rope that had been soaked in salt, ague, and vervain and began to bind Noxx tightly. Malachi knew what worked to drain or dim a witch's magic from his own experience as a prisoner, and Ridge understood what a major extension of trust it was for Malachi to share that information.

Ridge set Noxx up in a chair, made sure to empty his pockets and remove any jewelry, and set down a circle of those same elements around the chair. Once Henri was in position to keep watch, Kane made his way over.

"Well. I can't say I pictured him quite like this," Kane observed.

Ridge nodded in agreement. For all that Noxx had been Letwick's magical inquisitor, the man himself didn't impress at first glance. Slender and of medium height, with a sharp-featured face framed by long gray hair, Noxx was remarkably average.

To Ridge's Sight, the stain on Noxx's soul from swearing loyalty to a dark mage had spread, making him hideous to behold.

"How long until he wakes up?" Ridge restrained his urge to stab Noxx to get a response. He wanted vengeance.

"Should be any moment now," Kane replied. He held a long knife, similar to the one Ridge had pulled from the scabbard on his belt.

Noxx groaned and rolled his head drunkenly. His eyes struggled open, then worked to focus, and his body jerked against the ropes until he realized he was restrained. He paid no attention to Henri, gave Kane a confused once-over, but when his gaze settled on Ridge, his expression shifted to recognition—and hatred.

"You." Venom dripped from his tone. "The other Shadow."

"We have questions," Ridge managed to say in a cold, impartial voice, sinking into his role as an assassin to hold himself together.

"I bet you do," Noxx replied in a gravelly voice. He sounded slightly drunk, but Malachi had assured him the witch was capable of answering the questions, and the drugs lowered both inhibitions and mental defenses. The man's skin had a sickly gray cast, his eyes were deeply shadowed, and his angular face looked haggard.

"We know the Witch Lord set you up with Duke Letwick as his advisor—and spy," Ridge said, refusing to let Noxx bait him into an argument. "And you abandoned him when his luck turned. What was in it for you?"

Noxx regarded him with a leer. "The question you should be asking is how to pick up the pieces of your partner's broken mind. Letwick told me that the potions I supplied were quite effective—but he always came back for something even stronger." He shook his head in false sympathy. "You can't fix him, after all that. If he's not dead yet, you might as well put him down like a mad dog." Even the drugs didn't blunt Noxx's penchant for cruelty or hide his lack of remorse.

"Don't need your opinion on that," Ridge said dismissively and took cold amusement in seeing Noxx look uncertain. "I'm interested why you hated the king enough to plot his death."

Noxx's lips twisted into a snarl. "Kristoph. That arrogant son of a whore. He deserved to die. I hope it was slow and painful."

"What did he do? Take your land? Seize your gold? He didn't force you into his service, or you couldn't have been in Letwick's employ," Ridge replied.

Noxx began to laugh, a slow, unhinged chuckle that sent ice down Ridge's spine. "What does it matter? He's dead. Letwick's dead—I sensed it. Were you the one to do it? Did you enjoy it?"

Ridge bit back a comment and restrained himself from backhanding the witch. "Answer the question."

"The Witch Lord took me in when I was broken, when I'd lost everything, and gave me purpose. I repaid him willingly with my service."

"Duke Letwick served the Witch Lord, but I guess Makary's loyalty only runs one way because he sure didn't show up to save Letwick before I slit his throat." Ridge wasn't surprised to see that his words barely got a flinch out of Noxx.

"Letwick failed. He knew the penalty."

"But Makary didn't take you with him," Ridge pointed out. "Left you high and dry."

"I didn't need his help."

"Because it's turned out so well on your own?" Ridge couldn't help a petty thrill at the glint of anger in Noxx's eyes.

"What do you want to hear? That we both failed? We did. I thought that blustering fool could carry out easy instructions, but he and his idiot chirurgeon couldn't manage to do one simple thing right," Noxx spat.

"Letwick failed you. The Witch Lord left you to die. Don't you want to make him pay?"

Noxx regarded Ridge with glazed eyes. "What did you have in mind?" The drugs slurred his words.

"How is he controlling the regency council candidates? Threats? Blackmail? Intimidation?"

Noxx's unpleasant laugh made Ridge's stomach tighten.

"Nothing that complicated. The Witch Lord arranged for each member of the council to receive a gift. The objects are bespelled, a curse on the owner to make them more pliable, easier to bend to his will."

"How do we break the curse—or the connection?"

"Let me go, and I'll tell you."

"Tell us, and I'll end you quickly," Ridge countered, in no mood for games.

Maybe Noxx saw a glint of madness in Ridge's gaze, or perhaps the assassin's reputation preceded him. The bound mage lifted his chin to stare down Ridge as he answered. "We both know that no matter what I do, you're going to kill me anyway."

"Up to you how that goes."

"I wanted to destroy Kristoph because he's the reason my daughter is dead." Noxx tilted his head, clearly curious about Ridge's response.

"Go on."

Hatred twisted Noxx's features, but this time it was shadowed by sorrow. "One summer, when they were both just sixteen, my daughter met Kristoph—long before he took the throne. I'm a Letwick cousin, so we were included in the event. It was a hunting party at one of the lodges. And while the men went off with the horses and dogs, the families ate and drank and gamed and gossiped.

"Calia was smitten, and the prince seemed to return her interest. We thought it was just a harmless flirtation. They spent two weeks together in a whirlwind, and none of the rest of us realized how serious it had become."

Noxx looked away as if the pain of the memory overrode even the dire circumstances of his confession. "The king's minders suddenly noticed that the prince had been keeping company with a girl who wasn't a suitable marriage prospect. They forced him to leave without a farewell, and despite whatever promises they made, she didn't hear from him again."

Noxx's former belligerence yielded to bitter grief. "In the weeks that followed, Calia stopped eating. She took to her bed and wouldn't be consoled. And then one day, she threw herself off the highest tower."

His head snapped back to face Ridge, and how the mage's glazed eyes burned with hatred. "Kristoph cost me my daughter, and her life meant nothing to him. He went back to his palace and the parade of 'suitable' prospects while my Calia was cold in her grave. Right then, I decided that somehow I would make him pay."

Ridge looked at Noxx, a man so twisted with grief that destroying a kingdom seemed like a reasonable recompense for his loss.

"I'd say you have your vengeance against Kristoph—many times over," Ridge said. "But what about the Witch Lord? Yefim Makary used you, leveraged your pain to make you his pawn, and then abandoned you. How is Calia's memory avenged if Makary becomes the power behind the throne with the Regency Council?"

Noxx focused on Ridge. "I'm dying. Worked a spell with Makary, and it went wrong. Sorry to take the fun out of executing me. So—sure. I'll tell you how to stop Makary. Might as well burn everything down on my way out."

Ridge suspected that Noxx hadn't told the whole truth about what happened to his daughter, but he also didn't doubt that the witch was very sick.

"How do we break the Witch Lord's control over the regency council candidates?" he repeated.

Noxx stared at him for a moment, silent until Ridge finally decided the witch didn't intend to answer. Then Noxx licked his dry lips and gave him a smile that showed his teeth.

"Makary had a big piece of garnet that anchored his control ritual. He made the 'gifts' for the council from that original piece. Carved each one into the shape of an eye—told them it would bring them insight and wisdom to rule the kingdom."

Noxx snorted in derision. "The fools never questioned it. Not even when Makary told them to always keep the eye with them and to sleep with it beneath their pillows. He promised them all kinds of protections. Lies—all lies."

His tongue flicked over cracked lips, reminding Ridge of a snake. "Break the anchor stone, and his control through the pieces also shatters. Since Letwick was an accomplice—and related—Makary hid the anchor in the manor."

"Where?" Ridge pressed.

Noxx's breath hitched, and deep, wracking coughs shook his body. Blood flecked his lips. "Told you I'm dying," he said when he looked up to find Kane and Ridge staring.

"The anchor is wrapped in spelled cloth in a secret room on the second floor of the mansion."

"Is it protected?" Kane asked, sounding like he suspected a trap.

"Yes," Noxx rasped. "And the room will only open for him—or me."

Kane cursed under his breath. Ridge's temper flared, and he struggled to rein in his anger. Kane and Ridge retreated to a corner of the room.

"I should have known Noxx would set another trap, damn him," Kane said.

"Question is—has he told the truth about anything? Is it worth the risk to find out?" Ridge replied.

Despite his reservations, Ridge also saw an opportunity. With Letwick dead and disgraced, the family had fled the mansion to go into hiding. The servants probably left when the food ran out. There would never be a better opportunity to steal the anchor—assuming Noxx's information was good.

"I can believe Makary suckered him in with promises and then betrayed him—that's how he works," Kane said. "And it's not a stretch that Noxx could sell out Makary for revenge."

"But he'd also happily lead us to our deaths with an offer he knows we won't turn down," Ridge pointed out.

Kane shot a look toward their prisoner. "Let's take him with us. He's drugged, and we can keep him that way. He said only he or Makary can open the room. If it's a trap, he'll be in front. If he lied to us, we've got no reason to keep him alive."

"That works." He and Kane walked back toward Noxx together.

"Change of plans," Ridge announced. "You're going to lead us to the hidden room and open it, then give us the garnet and tell us how to destroy it."

"And then you kill me." Noxx looked away. "No thanks."

"We could kill you—clean, quick, final. Or we take you to a necromancer I know, and he could see how often you could be killed and resurrected before you started coming back defective," Kane mused with horrifying detachment.

Ridge and Henri exchanged a look, hoping Kane wasn't telling the truth.

Noxx regarded Kane through narrowed eyes, probably trying to figure out the same thing. He licked his lips nervously. "Sounds unpleasant. Save that for Makary," he added with a hoarse chuckle. "Seeing how I don't have much choice, you've got a deal."

"Anything we need to know about moving the anchor?" Kane asked, suspicion clear in his tone.

"Don't touch the garnet barehanded," Noxx replied, pausing for another fit of coughing. "The spelled cloth amplifies its power."

"How do we break the spell and destroy the anchor?" Ridge had no intention of taking Noxx completely at his word, but he also could imagine Makary being overconfident enough to discount Letwick as a threat.

"The spell itself is fairly simple. Crush the garnet and cast the cloth and the shards into a hot fire. The connection will break, and the regency council candidates will be free."

Ridge looked for the catch. "Did you help Makary work the spell that bound the anchor to the pieces used for the gifts?"

Noxx drew breath to speak and ended up coughing. When he lifted his head to answer, defiance still burned in his eyes despite his failing health.

"Stupidly, yes. I thought it was an honor," Noxx replied bitterly. "But the working required more power than Makary chose to spare of his own, so he took mine. By the time I realized what was happening, it was too late."

Ridge gave him an appraising look. "Let me guess—he not only depleted your power, but it broke other spells you had worked on yourself. Ones that kept you from aging or held back whatever's killing you."

"I was a fool. He wanted me out of the way—a reminder of the failure to put Letwick on the throne—so he could move on with his new plan."

"What happens when the garnet shatters?" Kane asked.

"The energy of the spell releases," Noxx replied. "Or so Makary said."

"Let's get going before we lose the light." Kane crossed through the warded circle and jammed a drug-tipped arrow into the meat of Noxx's shoulder, delivering another dose of potion.

"What was that?" Noxx yelped.

"Insurance," Kane replied, jerking the bound witch to his feet.

Henri checked to make sure the manor house was empty, then signaled for the others to enter. Ridge led the way, followed by Kane, who was manhandling Noxx, and Henri bringing up the rear.

"Where's this hidden room?" Kane asked, giving Noxx a shake.

"Second floor, last room on the left—it's a parlor. Secret door is next to the fireplace." Noxx sounded drunk from the fresh dose, but Ridge didn't trust the witch not to double-cross them, no matter how delirious and weakened he might be. From the set of Kane's jaw, the spy agreed.

The manor appeared to have been hastily abandoned. The mess left behind suggested to Ridge that the occupants had been given minutes to pack whatever they could carry and flee, leaving everything else behind. It didn't look like looters had gotten to the manor yet, and the house was undamaged. Ridge wondered if Letwick's family ever intended to return.

The well-appointed parlor befitted a nobleman with dark wood wainscoting, heavy mahogany furnishings, oil paintings of hunting scenes, and a massive, carved mantle over the fireplace.

Kane gave Noxx a shove toward the corner. "You said you had to be the one to open the secret door. Get to it."

Noxx splayed his hand over the center of a wooden panel and murmured words under his breath. Even with his drug-weakened magic, the spell responded. They heard a click, and then a narrow door swung open.

Henri lit a lantern from a nearby table and held it aloft to light the way.

"You, first." Kane prodded Noxx with the tip of his knife. Noxx stepped into the small space while Kane and Ridge blocked the entrance, and Henri turned to watch the main door, in case the mansion wasn't as deserted as they thought.

The secret room was barely the size of a closet. Shelves covered three walls, leaving barely enough space for two men to stand shoulder-to-shoulder in the middle.

"That's it—in the box," Noxx said, pointing with his bound hands to a medium-sized wooden chest carved with sigils. "That's got the garnet in it—and the blackmail material Makary kept as a surety in case the magic failed. Everything you need to destroy his candidates for the Regency Council."

"Open it," Ridge ordered.

Noxx glared at him, but he lifted the lid and held the box out awkwardly, constrained by his bonds. Inside, Ridge saw a large chunk of garnet, a cloth embroidered with more symbols, and a stack of papers. "It's all there—just like I said."

Noxx threw the box at Ridge and Kane, darted back into the closet, and tried to slam the door. Ridge stopped it from closing with his boot, but Noxx sent something flying through the opening that hit the floor and filled the parlor with stinking smoke.

Ridge and Kane stayed shoulder to shoulder, blocking the doorway to the hidden room, making sure Noxx couldn't get past them even as they choked and struggled to breathe, tears streaming down their faces.

Henri broke a window, and the fresh air quickly cleared the room. Ridge slammed the door to the secret closet open—but Noxx was gone.

"Fuck! Where did he go?" Kane thundered.

Ridge fell to his knees and felt along the floorboards until he found a hidden latch. He yanked open the trapdoor, and the lantern showed them a ladder descending into darkness.

"He can't have gone far." Ridge moved to follow Noxx down the ladder. He cursed himself that he hadn't realized Noxx wasn't as drugged as he'd let on.

Kane grabbed him by the arm and refused to let Ridge shake off his hand. "Let him go."

Ridge rounded on the spy, furious. "Are you kidding? After what he did to Rett?"

"Noxx knows what's down there. You don't. He's probably hoping you'll follow so he can make an easy kill. There could be a warren of passageways and more than a few traps. I'm not going to explain to Rett that I let you die."

"He played us," Ridge growled.

"But he also gave us the garnet and the blackmail information to stop Makary's council choices from being confirmed." Kane pointed out. "He just managed to save his own skin at the same time."

Ridge jerked free of Kane's hold, but he headed back to the main room while Kane kicked the trapdoor shut. "We had him—and he got away. We were fools."

"His story made sense," Kane replied, sounding calm, although Ridge could tell from the set of the other man's jaw that the mercenary was angry too. "Most of it might have been true. Makary probably did sucker Noxx into working with him to drain his energy and make him less of a threat."

While they argued, Henri quietly went about the business of cleaning up. He used a fireplace poker to nudge spilled items back into the sigil box and close the lid. Then he tore open a pillow, dumped out the stuffing, and got the box inside without touching it, lifting it with a grin. "Ready to go."

"Noxx thought he was helping bring the Regency Council under the Witch Lord's control, when in reality, Makary was controlling him too. He saw a chance to use us to avenge himself on Makary," Kane said.

Ridge paced, fists clenched, trying to walk off his anger. *Noxx might have gotten payback on Makary, but he owes me for Kristoph and Rett. This isn't over until Noxx is dead—and Makary too.*

CHAPTER SEVEN

"You blew up the bridge?" Rett knew he shouldn't have been surprised—after all, they'd taken Henri with them—but hearing about the adventure made everything feel different than being there.

"It worked," Henri replied with a shrug.

"Of course, we had to go twenty miles out of our way to get home because there wasn't another bridge closer," Kane noted.

"But we did get back," Ridge pointed out.

Rett and the others gathered at the table in Rune Keep around a dinner of hearty onion soup, freshly baked bread, cheese, and figs. Malachi had a bottle of whiskey on the table, and they toasted another day they all survived.

Rett hung back, listening intently as Ridge, Kane, and Henri took turns recounting their adventure. They made a good team. Even though Noxx got away, breaking the Witch Lord's hold on the regency council candidates mattered, and they still didn't know what was in the spelled box. Rett was just grateful none of them had been hurt.

Their success didn't ease the discomfort he felt hearing about the job as a bystander. Deep down, Rett couldn't help feeling replaced.

It doesn't change anything. Kane needs a hunting partner who can leave the tower more often than Malachi dares. Ridge needs someone to have his back who isn't going to get lost in his own head. Ridge and I still have a lifetime of being best friends. Kane and Malachi are together.

The new hunting team didn't change anything—except that it did.

"Provided Noxx told the truth about the garnet, I'll figure out how to smash it, and that should break Makary's hold on the candidates for the Regency Council," Malachi recounted. "Meanwhile, Rett and I paid another visit to Brother Tom."

Ridge looked sharply at Rett. "You left the tower?" Rett knew that worry made his partner's tone sharp and angry. His head swiveled, and he glared at Malachi. "You let him leave?"

"We stayed here," Rett assured him, eager to make peace. "At least, physically."

Ridge's eyes widened. "You soul-traveled?"

"You did your part; I did mine. Malachi came along for the ride, so it wasn't all on me. We were fine."

"I'd say it was well worth the effort," Malachi interposed, no doubt sensing the rising tension. He started to recount what they learned at Green Knoll, with Rett picking up pieces of the story as they went along.

"You're sure Brother Tom is real?" Kane glanced from Rett to Malachi and back again.

"How is that even possible?" Ridge demanded.

Rett's temper flared. "You think the crazy guy made it up? I have a witness. Malachi saw everything."

"I don't think you're crazy—"

"Just too damaged to know what's real and what isn't?" Rett threw down the challenge, satisfied when Ridge flinched.

"That isn't—"

"It's exactly what you meant," Rett snapped. "If you don't trust me, then trust Malachi."

"What do you think of the visit to Brother Tom?" Kane put in, an unlikely peacekeeper. The set of his jaw suggested that he'd have words with Malachi in private about the risk, but he seemed to sense that diffusing the tension was essential.

"Not sure yet, but there's serious magic involved," Malachi replied. "That's one of the most extensive occult libraries I've seen. The energy required to create a place *between* is something that would take a very powerful—or desperate—mage."

"Kristoph didn't have a witch that strong except for you," Rett countered, with a nod toward Malachi.

"And we know how that turned out," Malachi said ruefully.

"But this rift … it's not something you could do, is it?" Kane looked to Malachi, curious and worried.

Malachi shook his head. "No. I'm going to have to do a lot of research to even guess at how it might have been done. I think that's going to be important because I have a strong sense that we're going to have to preserve it for now—and eventually, undo it."

"You think there are people living somewhere that isn't here and isn't somewhere else?" Ridge asked, looking baffled.

Malachi chuckled. "I'm not sure I'd put it quite that way. But, yes."

"Who are they? Why are they there? It seems like a lot of effort just to hide some books."

"We agree," Rett replied, tamping down on his irritation with Ridge enough to rejoin the conversation. "Brother Tom seems to be the likely focus. But he was an orphan, like us. If he's unusual, he doesn't know it. He came to the monks as a child, so he's not a prisoner."

"Assuming he told you the truth," Kane pointed out.

"I didn't sense a falsehood," Malachi replied. "At least, as far as Brother Tom knew."

"What if you went there and couldn't get back?" Ridge sounded more worried about their soul travel than if they'd gone into full battle.

"That didn't happen," Rett countered.

Ridge's glower made it clear that the dispute wasn't over. Rett wasn't ready to let it rest.

"Every battle is a risk," Rett argued. "But we still go. I didn't travel alone; I didn't go without preparation. I was with one of the most powerful witches in the kingdom. We are in a place that's probably more secure than the king's palace. We're assassins. It's not our business to be safe."

The temperature in the room dropped, and both Rett and Malachi looked up, turning toward the same area as Edvard's ghost appeared.

"Noxx did not tell you the whole truth about his daughter's death."

Malachi relayed Edvard's words for the benefit of Ridge and Kane.

"Where is the lie?" Kane asked.

"There is more to the story than has been said. Lorella and Lady Sally Anne suspected as much. Noxx's daughter's spirit is willing to talk to you," Edvard replied.

The ghost of a young woman took shape beside him. She wore a dress befitting someone of noble birth, and her dark hair was plaited with pearls and strands of gold. Rett's heart broke when he realized how young she was—just sixteen summers, far too young to die so tragically.

"I'll lend the ghosts the energy to make themselves seen and heard to everyone," Malachi said.

"I am Calia, daughter of the man you know as Noxx. Edvard has told me what my father said. He was a bad man, willing to betray anyone for his own gain. Even me."

Rett glanced at Ridge and Kane, but it was clear that Malachi's necromancy enabled them to hear the ghost as clearly as Rett did.

"We are sorry to trouble your rest," Rett said in a gentle tone. "But Edvard believes your story is important. Please, tell us what happened."

"My father had one love—power. He was Duke Letwick's witch, but he wished to be elevated to the king's court. At the hunting party, he realized that Prince Kristoph and I were of an age, and he did everything he could to push us together."

"Romantically?" Kane asked.

Calia nodded. "The prince was handsome and intelligent. He found me attractive. But the relationship between us happened so fast; I wondered later if a spell was involved.

"Father filled my head with silly notions of winning Kristoph's heart and becoming queen. I was young and loved to hear the bards sing songs about brave, faithful lovers. By the time the hunting party ended, I was pregnant with Kristoph's child, although I didn't know it at the time," Calia recounted.

Ridge watched the ghost intently. "Did Kristoph know?"

"When I realized what had happened, I panicked. I was afraid of what my parents would say, and I wanted to go to my lover. I didn't want to tell anyone until I could share the news with him. But my maid betrayed me and told my mother. She didn't believe the child belonged to the prince, but I hadn't been with any other man," Calia told them, sad and somber, in a tone heavy with grief.

"My mother raged at me and called me terrible things. Then Father found out, and he believed me—but instead of carrying a message to my prince, he locked me in a room and kept my situation a secret from all but my mother and the maid," she continued.

"I wrote a letter to Kristoph and paid one of the servants to bribe a merchant to take it to the palace. I didn't know whether the note would reach him, but it took a weight off my heart to know that I'd tried." Calia stopped and took a moment to collect herself.

"I never heard back from Kristoph and figured the letter didn't reach the palace. The whole time I was with child, I remained locked in my room. But I told myself that I would have the baby to love, and someday we would go to the palace together." She stopped and bowed her head, overcome with grief. Edvard laid an ephemeral hand on her shoulder.

"Something went wrong," Malachi guessed, looking as angry about Noxx's betrayal as Rett felt.

Calia nodded, then straightened her shoulders and went on. "The birth was difficult, but my son and I survived. I named him Toland and dreamed of presenting him to the prince. But we only had a few weeks together. One night, a priest and a group of monks came."

Her expression grew fierce. "They ripped my baby from my arms, and the priest told me that they were under orders from the king—Kristoph's father—to kill Toland so there could be no pretender to the throne."

Ferocity gave way to a haunted look. "I pleaded and begged, but the priest wouldn't listen. Even Father's anger and attempts at bribery made no difference. The priest took my baby to kill him," Calia repeated. "I watched from my window as they rode away. I had lost everything. Kristoph cared nothing for Toland and me, my child was gone, and as I heard Father try to bargain with the priest, I realized that he cared more about his place at court than about me or my baby."

Her voice grew cold and distant. "I had no reason left to live. That night, when the maid came, I hit her over the head and ran out, climbed to the top of the tower, and threw myself off."

"Why did your spirit stay?" Malachi prompted. "You could have gone to your rest."

"Not without my child." Calia's eyes sparked with fury. "I have been searching for his spirit all these years. I can't rest until we're together again."

"Thank you for telling your story," Rett said, his throat tight with emotion.

"Help me find my baby. Please, I beg of you. Use your magic to give us both our final peace."

"I will do whatever is in my power to help," Malachi promised. "You have my word."

"And mine," Rett echoed.

"Thank you," Calia's ghost replied. "That is more than I dared to hope." With that, both Calia and Edvard's images faded, leaving the room silent.

"That son of a bitch," Ridge growled, slamming his fist down on the table.

"I had the feeling he wasn't telling us everything—of course he wasn't—but I didn't think he'd lie about his daughter," Kane said, sounding equally angry. "Especially when he blamed Kristoph for her death and said that was why he helped Letwick kill the king."

Malachi tapped his fingers on the table as he thought. "Perhaps from Noxx's perspective, there was a certain kind of sense to it. He manipulated Calia and Kristoph—possibly bespelled them—to ensure she bore his child, an heir to the throne of Landria.

"Maybe he thought Kristoph was truly besotted with her and would marry Calia, or at least elevate Noxx among his advisors. When Kristoph refused to acknowledge Calia—and

King Renvar had the baby murdered—Noxx overlooked his role in the tragedy and wanted vengeance on Kristoph."

"For crushing his own ambition, not for what it cost his daughter," Kane muttered.

"Is it possible to find a baby's ghost?" Rett asked, looking to Malachi. "How could it be done for a child too young to know its name?"

Malachi shook his head. "I don't know. I've never had reason to look, although Calia surely isn't the first grieving parent to want to be reunited. I'll have to study the lore."

"Ironic, isn't it?" Kane said, with an edge in his voice. "Kristoph's first son—a bastard—is murdered by royal decree, and his second is stillborn. Maybe the gods were finished with them and their dynasty."

"We don't know that Kristoph ever received Calia's letter," Rett mused. "Only that she sent it, and the priest came." He looked to Malachi. "Kristoph exiled you because you couldn't save his wife and son. Did you think his grief was false?"

Malachi remained silent for a moment. "No. He was out of his mind, completely bereft. Since he was unable to punish the gods, he lashed out at a convenient substitute—me. I can't forgive him for costing me my freedom, but a part of me understands him. I didn't doubt in the moment that he was grief-stricken, and over the years I've had to reflect, I've never changed that opinion."

Rett nodded. "Exactly. Kristoph had his faults. But I can't imagine that he'd want the child dead, even if the connection he had to Calia was from a love spell. At that age, he might not have wanted the responsibility of fatherhood, but there were plenty of servants to care for the baby. The fear of a pretender wouldn't be a reason to do murder for a teenage prince. I think that Renvar alone ordered the death and that Kristoph likely knew nothing about it."

"What's your point?" Ridge asked, still too angry to temper the bite in his tone.

"I think Kristoph's father feared a plot—which was wise, considering what we know of Noxx and the Letwicks—and took steps to protect the line of succession. If Kristoph ever asked about Calia or learned of the child, it would have been easy for his father to tell him that she, and the baby, died in childbirth," Rett replied.

He met Malachi's gaze. "That would make his grief all the more extreme when to his mind, the same loss happened 'again.'"

"Shit," Kane muttered, looking to Malachi. "Makes a damn good theory."

Malachi looked poleaxed as the possibility sank in. "So Noxx set in motion the reason for my life sentence?"

Rett nodded. "We certainly didn't know Kristoph well, but from what we saw of him, sending someone to kill the child doesn't fit."

"We need to find out more." Malachi rose and went to the window. After a moment, the ghostly shape of a large raven appeared. He spoke quietly with the apparition and then watched it wing away.

"You sent him to Gil?" Kane asked, raising an eyebrow.

Malachi nodded. "Gil has the connections—and the blackmail material—to encourage people to share what they'd rather not remember. Kristoph was only in his early forties when he died, so the affair with Calia would have been about twenty-five years ago. Plenty of nobles who might remember should still be alive, maybe even some who were at that hunting party."

Kane chuckled. "Gil is going to sink his teeth into that kind of assignment. Nice juicy scandal. Luc might be able to pick up some old rumors among the military men. Nothing ever stays as much of a secret as people would like to think—especially when it's good for gossip."

"I also asked Gil to find out more about Runcian, Kristoph's father's witch. If the old king was willing to have his grandson put to death, he and his witch probably made a lot of other, equally horrific, decisions. Perhaps part of Kristoph's dislike of mages came from personal experience—and not just his anger at me," Malachi mused. "I suspect that, if they hear about any impact on the regency council candidates, he'll tell us."

Rett looked quizzically at Malachi. "What are you thinking?"

Malachi shrugged, and Rett guessed that the other man had not yet cast off his mood from Calia's story. "I never had a reason to look into Runcian before. Surely there are records—and tales. If I can learn more about his magic, that may be useful."

"Depending on when the manuscripts and books were moved into Green Knoll, we might find some records there," Rett suggested.

Ridge glowered. "It's not a good enough reason for you to go back. What if you get stuck?"

"What if I can find something that helps us finish the Witch Lord, once and for all?" Rett countered.

Ridge looked away. "Too much risk for an 'if.'"

Rett looked around, realizing that Henri had slipped out. *Damn, he can move like a ghost when he wants to.* "Where's Henri?"

"I gave him a list of what I'll need for my next workings and asked him to pull the items to see what we might be missing. I suspect he's in the storeroom," Malachi replied.

Rett felt the events of the day catch up with him. The satisfying food and excellent whiskey had given him a warm glow, and despite the many unsettled issues, he felt good that they had made progress.

"I'm going to bed," he announced as he stood. "Just tell me if you come up with something else for me to do."

Rett reached the room he shared with Ridge and took a few deep breaths, needing a moment of quiet. He tried not to feel overwhelmed by the swirling mysteries and the fact that the Witch Lord and Noxx were still free.

He wasn't surprised when Ridge followed him moments later.

"I don't want to fight," Ridge blurted, hands raised, palms out in appeasement. "I know I might not have sounded like that out there, but honestly, I'm scared. I don't understand the soul traveling. I remember how close to death you were when we rescued you from Letwick and what it's taken to get you back to where you are now. I just don't want to see you like that all over again."

Ridge's confession came out in a breathless rush. Rett and Ridge had always been able to talk to each other and didn't make a habit of keeping secrets, so they rarely had to have a fraught discussion. They'd worked and lived together so long that they were normally in tune with one another, and their skills and abilities—until now—were similar enough that arguments were rare.

For Ridge to admit his fear about Rett's expanded magic took effort and courage, and Rett appreciated the gesture.

He strained to keep his temper in check because he couldn't shake the feeling that some of Ridge's protectiveness sprang from doubting Rett's decisions.

"I don't want to die," Rett replied, hoping his exhaustion didn't make him snappish. "But you've always trusted me before. Why don't you trust me now?"

Ridge looked like he'd been punched. "I never said I didn't trust you. I've always trusted you—with my life."

"We never doubted that going out on a job would be dangerous. That never stopped us. My body isn't ready yet to go back to the physical fight—although I'm getting closer," Rett continued.

"I know." Ridge's expression told Rett he was still trying to stand his ground without causing another argument. "But I almost lost you. I thought you were dead, and I couldn't handle it. Then Malachi either brought you back or helped you hang on, and I was just so damn glad that you weren't gone. Putting yourself in danger in a way I don't understand and can't follow—I don't think I'll make it if you get yourself killed."

"I'm sorry that I scared you. I'd feel the same if things were reversed. But I can't stop the visions and dreams," Rett argued. "Malachi is teaching me ways to lessen their impact, but that doesn't always work. Maybe they'll stop—but perhaps this is the new me, with the lid blown off those abilities for good. If I can't make them go away, there might be a way I can make them into a weapon." Rett tried to make his case and hoped he could persuade Ridge. He felt heartened that Ridge was still listening, but he knew how stubborn his partner was and how deep his protective streak went.

"A weapon—how?"

"Before Letwick, my visions saved our asses more than once, warning of danger. If that ability is stronger now, maybe I can learn to channel it. Focus on something hidden that we need to find, or a secret that we need to know."

"It's not the visions I'm worried about," Ridge admitted. "It's you, going traveling without your body. What if you get lost? What if you can't get back into your body? We already have Edvard spying for us, and Malachi can call up other ghosts to help. I just don't want you to *be* a ghost."

Rett sat on his bed and leaned his elbows on his knees, head in his hands. "I'm sidelined here in the tower until I get my strength back. That's the right thing to do because I don't want my weakness to get anyone killed. And I can see how well you and Henri work with Kane. He's good. If I had to be replaced—"

"Replaced?" Ridge echoed, and his calm facade slipped, anger glinting in his eyes. "Who said anything about being *replaced?* That's not what this is about."

"Maybe it should be. I don't know if I can be fixed."

"Stop it! We've already had this discussion. I don't want to go through it again," Ridge snapped. "You're my best friend. That hasn't changed. Yes, Kane's good—but he likes to work alone. This is temporary, so we can run down leads outside the tower while you and Malachi look into the kinds of things we can't. I am counting on having my original partner back. So can we be done with the whole 'replaced' idea?"

Rett grimaced. "See—this is all part of the aftermath. Everything runs closer to the surface than before—magic, emotions, memories. It's like trying to think while there's a band playing and someone is shouting in your ear, and fireworks are going off."

"All the more reason for you to be here while you sort through it, with Malachi to help," Ridge said, looking tired now that the anger drained away. "Does he think the changes are permanent?"

Rett hesitated, then shook his head. "He doesn't know for sure, but he says either I'll learn to deal with it, or the overwhelming parts will gradually go away." He looked up at Ridge. "But you need me *now*."

Ridge shook his head and gave him a look of fond exasperation.

"Yes—I need you now, safe and well. Everything you're doing matters," Ridge assured him. "But letting your body heal is the most important because that's how you're going to get back out there with Henri and me. Where you belong."

CHAPTER EIGHT

"He found them again—Burke and Caralin," Rett said.

Rett didn't open his eyes when he spoke. He lay on the bed, probably feeling the ache in his head pulse in time with his heartbeat, Ridge guessed.

A vision sent from Sofen usually laid Rett out for a couple of candlemarks. Rett had told him that the young psychic had tremendous power but lacked subtlety. That meant that the images hit like a sledgehammer, leaving Rett feeling like his skull might split in two.

Ridge put a cool cloth across Rett's eyes and hoped it soothed the ache. "That potion of Malachi's should take effect soon," Ridge said. Rett grunted in reply.

"Burke and Caralin are still safe?" Ridge asked.

"As much as any of us are. The Shadows that remained loyal to Kristoph are with them," Rett answered, pressing the cold, wet compress against his eyes.

"How many?"

"Not nearly enough."

"Shit."

Ridge and Rett had rescued Sofen from slavers who were kidnapping orphans with foresight or other supernatural, paranormal abilities. The Witch Lord had been behind the network of slavers who placed the psychic children with his loyalists so that they could pass covert messages and ferret out information.

When Ridge and Rett broke up the kidnapping ring, they managed to spirit the children away to Lady Sally Anne's fortified haven at Harrowmont. Sofen had emerged as a leader among the children and used his abilities to draw others like them to safety.

While Sofen and the others were studying with older, more seasoned psychics in the safety of Harrowmont, he still hadn't learned to consistently adjust his power to ease the impact on the receiver.

Rett groaned. "Sofen packs a punch."

"I guess he's still working on not 'yelling,'" Ridge said. "Are you all right?"

"Compared to what?"

"Point taken." Ridge paused. "What are you thinking we should do with that information?"

"Noxx is still missing. Malachi's working out how to properly break Makary's garnet, but we don't know whether doing that will stop the regency council candidates from helping Makary take over the throne or just remove the Witch Lord's ability to compel them. We have the blackmail evidence, but it's no use without a way to get it to people we can trust in the palace. And then there's saving the monks in the 'between space.' We can't tell the Shadows about Green Knoll, and they haven't been much use tracking down Noxx, so I'm not sure what good it does to know where they are."

Inside the box with the garnet were notes, letters, lists of names, and dates, all information that incriminated the leading candidates for the Regency Council in Kristoph's death and linked people to the various schemes Ridge and Rett had foiled prior to the king's murder.

"It sounds like Makary wasn't taking any chances this time. He's done well before convincing greedy nobles to throw in their lot with him. Then he had the garnet to compel them and blackmail material if the magic failed. Maybe he's running out of ways to steal the throne," Ridge mused.

"The stuff in that box should be enough to discredit the entire council," Rett said.

"I'm not hopeful about that."

"Cynic."

"Let's see what Malachi hears back from Gil and Luc. I wish we didn't have to rely on ghost birds to pass messages back and forth," Ridge said.

"Gil's so valuable because he's still in the city, where we can't be," Rett pointed out.

"True. It's just that everything was complicated before Kristoph's death, and it's more so now," Ridge replied.

"We're safe. You and Henri and I are together. We've got allies. And food. Malachi's even got pretty decent whiskey. It could be a lot worse."

"I know. There's just so much that still isn't settled. Big stuff—like who's going to be king. The kinds of things we were never supposed to be involved in deciding," Ridge said. He patted Rett on the shoulder. "How about you sleep, and when Malachi hears from Gil, I'll wake you?" He paused. "Are we good with each other, you and me?"

"Yeah. Sorry for the temper."

"With everything you've been through, I'd say you get a pass on being a little cranky. But you don't have to worry—there's no one else I'd rather assassinate people with than you."

"Same here."

Ridge closed the door quietly behind him, hoping Rett would find a deep sleep that for once was peaceful.

"How is he?" Malachi looked up from his card game with Kane and Henri.

Ridge shrugged, knowing his mood was still off from before. "Visions give him a blinding headache, and since Sofen has to use a lot of power to send across such a distance, his 'messages' hit especially hard. I'm hoping whatever was in that tea you gave him will help."

"It should ease the pain," Malachi replied. "I didn't add anything to make him sleep because it would be worse to have nightmares and not be able to wake."

Ridge poured himself some whiskey and stood off to one side, watching the card game. "You've got to be careful playing against Henri," he warned. "He's a vicious card sharp."

Malachi grinned. "And I'm a necromancer, so if Henri cheats, I can have a ghost stand behind him and read his cards."

Kane snickered. "I've seen him do it. Be afraid."

Henri laid down a winning hand. "I don't need to cheat." He looked up at Ridge. "Winner gets the last apple tart. High stakes bidding."

Ridge sat as the others cleared the cards from the table and set out dotted bone tiles for a different game. "Sofen has located Burke and Caralin and the other loyal Shadows who are still with them."

"He was warning you where to avoid?" Kane wisecracked, only half in jest.

"Maybe they could get the Witch Lord's blackmail information on the council candidates to friends inside the palace," Ridge replied.

Kane sat back in his chair, looking thoughtful. "What makes you think they'd help you?"

"They might not. Certainly, no love lost between the other Shadows and Rett and me. Just because they're loyal to Kristoph doesn't mean they'd believe us about the Witch Lord being involved. Especially considering that he faked his own death," Ridge admitted.

"Awfully risky," Kane said. "And I'd hate to lose control of that evidence, especially to people who might like having you and Rett blamed for the king's death. On the other hand, Gil's father is an earl. Gil's known to Kristoph's former advisors—the ones who are still alive. If we can get the information to Gil, he and Luc will make sure it gets into the right hands."

"He's got a point," Henri agreed, absently nudging one of the bone tiles.

"Yeah," Ridge said, but the admission stung. "Just because we might be able to trust Burke and Caralin doesn't change anything with the others. And even Burke wanted to be assured that we didn't kill the king."

"Not a surprise that he needed to ask," Malachi said. "He's the Shadow Master—he wanted to judge his read on you answering the question."

Ridge muttered a curse under his breath. "Even without a palace or a king, we've got the same fucking politics that I always hated."

"I asked Gil to see what he could find out about the priest who took the baby from Calia. Dead or alive, I can search for him once we have a name," Malachi said. "I think there's more to the story than we've heard. More even than she knew."

"I have that feeling too," Ridge replied. "She was young and grief-stricken. But how did the priest know about the baby? Did her father try to make a deal that went sideways? Something doesn't add up."

"The ingredients Henri found for me will help to summon Kristoph's father, King Renvar. He bears the responsibility for this." Malachi's anger clear in his voice. "Kristoph's ghost might be bound, but I'd be surprised if the Witch Lord thought to bind the ghost of Kristoph's father."

"Did you know him?" Kane asked as Henri doled out the dotted bone tiles. That reminded Ridge that there was probably at least a few years age difference between Kane and Malachi.

"I wasn't seasoned enough to serve him as a witch," Malachi replied. "I was still apprenticed. But that allowed me to watch silently from the back of the room as my master served him. I was grateful that by the time I came into my full ranking, Kristoph was king."

Malachi shook his head, remembering. "King Renvar was hardened by wars that Kristoph didn't have to fight. The threats to Renvar's reign were military, while Kristoph's were political. Renvar's way of ruling belonged to a different time."

Malachi continued, "Kristoph was his own man. He viewed the world through different eyes than his father. That made him better-suited to his times, but perhaps less wary. Because of his father's ruthlessness, Kristoph inherited a kingdom ostensibly at peace—except for the traitors within."

"I can't imagine ordering the murder of his own grandson," Ridge said, shaking his head. "Yes, the baby was illegitimate, and I understand being wary of Noxx, but the child was still Kristoph's blood."

Kane met his gaze. "Have you read history? Much worse crimes have been committed by kings for even less potential gain."

Ridge listened for any noises that might suggest Rett's sleep was tormented, but the night passed quietly. *If he can rest, he can heal. He needs to know that I meant what I said. Kane's a decent stand-in, but I've got a lifetime of history with Rett.*

Around midnight, a ghostly vulture hunkered on the window sill, craning its neck and eyeing Malachi with a distressingly hungry gaze.

"Gil is so dramatic." Malachi sighed. He walked over, opened the window, and reached a hand out through the bars to touch the ghost-bird. His eyes closed as he focused on the message Gil sent via the spectral messenger. After a moment, he withdrew his hand, and the revenant faded.

Ridge and the others waited expectantly for Malachi to return to the table.

"Gil thinks he's identified the priest who took the baby and a location for him. He's old, so there's no telling how long he'll live. But he might be persuaded to tell us what really happened that night and whether they killed the baby."

"You doubt?" Kane looked up sharply.

Malachi frowned. "Murdering a bastard child is ruthless, although not without precedent. He might have had cause to suspect the Letwick clan were a threat, and the child would have been closely tied to that family since Noxx is a Letwick. King Renvar might have seen ordering the death to be a regrettable but necessary act to protect his succession. But while Renvar was cold, I didn't think him a monster. Practical, rational, and logical—yes. But amoral or heartless? That wasn't my impression at the time." He grimaced. "Then again, I was young and perhaps easily fooled."

"It's worth looking into," Kane agreed. "Because if the child didn't die, then there's an heir who has a closer consanguinity to the crown than anyone else, including Letwick's missing brother. We know what kind of king the Regency Council will choose if Makary is behind them."

"Do you really think the baby lives?" Ridge's voice dropped to a whisper as the implications flooded his mind.

"Until we know for certain, it's a possibility," Malachi replied. "We need to find out."

Ridge cast a guilty look at the bedroom door, then sighed and resigned himself to what had to happen. "If we've got a location, we should go as soon as we can to talk to the priest."

Kane raised an eyebrow. "Rett isn't going to like sitting out."

"I'm not sure about that. Sofen's vision walloped him. He's aware of his limitations right now," Ridge replied. "He just doesn't want to be replaced."

Kane snorted. "Seriously? Assure him he has nothing to worry about. You're fine in a fight and all, but definitely not my type." He reached over and took Malachi's hand.

Ridge rolled his eyes. "He returned his attention to Malachi. "Do you think you can summon King Renvar?"

Malachi nodded. "If he hasn't passed beyond the Veil, my power should compel his spirit. I think it would be … enlightening. But I also think that the three of you need to talk to the priest and get his perspective on what happened."

Gil's information was good, whatever his sources. Ridge, Henri, and Kane found themselves carefully riding on a poorly kept trail into the forest. Despite their initial concern that they had taken the wrong path, a small chapter house sat in a clearing at the end of the road, surrounded by a stone wall.

"I don't think they get a lot of visitors," Henri observed.

"I suspect that's the point," Kane said.

The one-story stone building had been weathered by time. Still, it looked sturdy enough, made from fieldstone and mortar. Neatly tended gardens surrounded it, along with a few fruit trees. A small barn stood along the edge of the clearing, with a fenced area that contained goats, sheep, and chickens.

"Not a very big place," Ridge said. "Can't be too many people living here."

"Do you think it's exile … or penance?" Henri asked.

"Guess we'll find out." Ridge nudged his horse to ride closer.

Kane hung back. He got down from his saddle and led his horse just behind the tree line, tethering him where branches provided a hiding place. The gesture indicated to Ridge and Henri that he intended to walk the perimeter and make sure they weren't disturbed.

Ridge and Henri looped their reins over an ancient hitching post before heading toward the door. Both men were armed, but Ridge sincerely hoped weapons weren't required.

Nothing marked the house as anything more than a private residence. Ridge wondered if the priest—Brother Sean—had left the monastic life. If he wanted solitude and contemplation, he'd picked the right location.

He knocked on the door. They waited, listening for movement inside. After a few minutes, Ridge and Henri exchanged a look. *Someone's obviously living here—or was until very recently. Are they ignoring us, or did something bad happen?*

Just as Ridge was about to break in, the door opened. A tall, hollow-cheeked man with deep-set eyes and a dour expression filled the doorway.

"Are you lost?" he asked. "The main road is just a few miles if you go right at the end of the lane."

Ridge couldn't tell if the directions were meant to be helpful or to hurry strangers off the property.

"We came here looking for Brother Sean," Henri replied with his most engaging smile.

The tall man took a half-step back with a shocked look on his face. "Who are you? What do you want?"

"Calia sent us," Ridge said and watched the color drain from the stranger's face.

"Come inside." The man glanced one way and the other, suddenly on guard.

They followed him into the house. The air smelled of cabbage and onions, and lamp smoke had turned the whitewashed walls light gray. Well-worn furnishings provided the basics—a table, three chairs near the fireplace, a wooden chest, and a bookshelf. A door led to a pantry on one side, while another opened into a hallway and presumably the sleeping rooms.

"Sit, if you must." The man gestured toward the chairs, but his welcome did not extend to offering refreshments.

Old habit had Henri standing where he could watch the hallway while Ridge stayed where he had a clear line of sight to the front door.

"Why have you troubled me? No one finds this house by accident," the man said. "And what do you know of Calia?"

Ridge studied him more closely, confirming that he was the right age to have been the man the ghost had described. He heard a note of fear in the man's voice, hidden beneath irascibility.

"Are you Brother Sean?" Ridge asked.

The gaunt man hesitated, then nodded. "That is the name I took when I entered the monastery many years ago. As you see, I no longer serve the priesthood. I am the caretaker to three elderly monks who live here with me. They are very hard of hearing and in their rooms, so our conversation will be private."

"Calia's ghost told us what happened the night you stole her child." Ridge couldn't resist a bit of satisfaction in the way Brother Sean flinched at the harsh truth. "Did you know that she killed herself shortly afterward because of what you did?"

Brother Sean nodded and looked down at his clasped hands. "I heard about her death much later. I knew in my heart that my actions were the cause."

"By whose orders did you take the child?" Ridge pressed. He wondered if the memory had weighed heavily on the old priest and whether their unpleasant conversation might offer confession if not absolution.

"My monks and I were sent at the order of King Renvar himself. He gave the charge to me in person, so there is no doubt of its origin."

"Why?"

Brother Sean looked up, but his gaze made it clear he was remembering the past. "He believed the child to be the illegitimate son of Prince Kristoph. His majesty did not approve of the union or the girl's family, and he feared the baby might someday challenge Kristoph for the throne."

"Calia was a cousin to the Letwicks, who were already in the distant line of succession," Ridge confirmed. "Her father was Duke Letwick's witch. Did you know that?"

Brother Sean shook his head. "Not at the time. Later, I wondered privately what the king feared more—a challenger or a witch."

"You told Calia that the child would be killed. Did that happen?" Too much was at stake for Ridge to gentle his inquiries. Brother Sean looked stricken, but he did not try to make them leave, and Ridge wondered if some relief came with the admission of guilt.

"That was my charge from the king. I was to 'take care' of the matter and bring him the child's severed hand as proof."

"What happened to the baby?"

Brother Sean swallowed hard. "Four men went with me that night—those among my brotherhood I trusted implicitly. None of us liked the assignment, but we were sworn to serve the king."

"What did you do?" Ridge felt a tingle down his spine, an inkling that things might not be what they seemed.

"The girl's father tried to bribe me to leave the child behind—concerned more with his own plans, I felt sure, than for his daughter and grandchild. But the girl sobbed and screamed and collapsed with such deep grief that it wounded my conscience," Brother Sean recalled.

"I feared the worst when I left with the child. I knew that the girl—Calia—I left sobbing on the floor would not go on without her baby and that she would receive no compassion from her father. I was stricken with guilt, and for the first time, I considered breaking my vows to the priesthood and my king."

Ridge remained quiet, feeling sure Brother Sean would continue his tale. After a moment in which he seemed to gather his composure, the former priest went on.

"I insisted on carrying the baby as we rode. He was very young, not even weaned. He shrieked at first, of course, when I took him from his mother. Then he settled and slept, only to wake bawling for milk. Of course, we had no provisions since the child was not supposed to survive. But since we had agreed to carry out our orders in the privacy of our chapter house, I stopped at a farm and bought a pail of milk. Then I dipped a clean rag into the liquid and let the child suck out the milk like from a teat."

Ridge's eyes narrowed, and he saw that Henri also looked skeptical. The monk's actions didn't sound like those of a man still committed to infanticide.

"We had been sworn to secrecy, so even our supervising priest didn't know the nature of our mission. Before we reached the cloister house, we stopped to confer. None of us wanted to carry out the order, but we knew we couldn't defy the dictate of the king. If we refused, we would be punished, and someone else would do what we could not."

Brother Sean sighed. "We came up with a plan to spirit the child away to a cousin of one of my men—somewhere far from the city. The baby would never know its parentage or come near the palace, and we could live with our consciences. But before we reached our destination, the king's witch, Runcian, blocked our way on the road."

Ridge raised an eyebrow when he met Henri's gaze; this was not the turn he had expected the story to take.

"Runcian knew of the king's order, and he guessed that we would not be willing to carry it through. He also had misgivings about killing the child, but for different reasons. He had an alternative and a way to keep the king from suspecting. So that's what we did."

"How did it work?" Ridge prompted.

"We feared the witch more than we feared the king, truth be told," Brother Sean recalled. "This was before magic was outlawed except for the priests and the army. I think at this point, none of us expected to survive, and we wondered if this was an elaborate test—which we failed."

He reached beneath his jacket for a flask and tipped it into his mouth before he continued. Ridge noticed that the old man's hands shook, but his eyes were clear and his voice steady. Ridge did not doubt his account or question his memory of the details. He suspected that the night had been a turning point in the priests' lives and not easily forgotten.

"The mage led us to this house, in the middle of nowhere, with a stolen sleeping baby, defying a direct order from the crown. I was so frightened that I nearly pissed myself," Brother Sean recounted.

"Runcian told us that he would provide an explanation to the king and to our superiors that would explain our absence. In the meantime, we were to remain on the grounds, never leave, receive no guests and send no messages. All our needs would be provided." Brother Sean's expression held a mix of fear and wonder.

"We did as we were told, and at first, we feared every day that either the king's troops or our chapter house brethren would descend on us. But as days and weeks became months and years, we realized that the witch had protected us somehow. We did not suspect the truth until much later."

"What truth?" Ridge pressed.

"One day, the witch came back. The boy—Toland—was almost two years old by then. The witch brought with him seven monks we did not recognize, men he said had sworn their lives to protect Toland, and that our part in this was done." He shook his head.

"That didn't go over well. We had grown fond of the boy—and besides, we had abandoned everything for him. Our vows, our role at the chapter house, our position with the king—it was all forfeit. Toland was *ours.*"

Brother Sean paused and looked from Ridge to Henri as if he expected them to doubt his word. "We protested. Whatever was to become of Toland, we had earned the right to be part of it. And the mage agreed—before he told us the rest of the plan.

"We would be missed if we disappeared forever. Questions would be asked, which might undo the precautions the mage had built while we raised Toland. I argued with him that we had already disappeared and abandoned our duties. Going back would only subject us to punishment—maybe even execution."

Ridge found that he was holding his breath, wondering how Brother Sean's story would conclude.

"Then the mage explained that he had hidden us and Toland in *time*. Somehow—I don't pretend to understand—he had changed how time worked here at the farm compared to outside. It had been two years for us. But out there ... it had been only a few days."

Brother Sean shrugged. "I have trouble explaining it. Saying it aloud sounds mad, I know. But everything the witch said was true. He told us that he intended to hide Toland and his hand-picked monks in a place 'outside of this world' where the king would never find him nor have reason to fear his return. As I understood it, time would progress in this outside realm, not like it had been standing still for us. The witch said he could not hold back time forever. We were to return with concocted evidence to show the king that we'd done the murder. Time moved ... but in truth only two *days* had gone by since we took Toland from his mother. The magic was that powerful."

Henri gasped. Brother Sean fixed Ridge with a look as if expecting denial, but Ridge was shocked into silence.

Shit. That's Green Knoll he's talking about. So that means Toland is Brother Tom. Kristoph's bastard son. The heir to the throne. Alive—and hidden.

"We doubted. But just to make sure, we stopped at an inn on our way back to the city. Runcian was right. To the outside world only days had passed, while here on the farm we had spent two years."

Henri frowned. "Does that mean it's going to be some-*when* different when we leave?"

"No." Brother Sean managed a wry smile. "That magic is long gone. If you hadn't guessed, the three men I care for were my partners in defying a royal order back then. We went back to our chapter house and kept the secret of Toland's existence for more than twenty years. The king's witch died. We never knew what became of Toland or if the witch had told us the truth, but we wanted to believe he was safe and well. We still hope that."

He paused, staring off into space. When he came back to himself, he went on. "We got old. By then, this house had been abandoned for quite a while. I volunteered to care for my friends and asked the chapter house to arrange for us to have this place as our retreat. We've been here ever since. One from our group died. For the rest of us, it is merely a matter of time."

Brother Sean fixed Ridge with a look. "Is that what you came for? I did not kill the baby. Knowing that my cruelty in the service of the king led to the death of an innocent girl has haunted me all these years. She and Toland deserved better. I couldn't save her—but we might have been able to save the boy. King Renvar was never the wiser, and to my knowledge, Kristoph never knew he had a son."

Ridge had been prepared to judge Brother Sean harshly for his actions, but the full story left him unsettled and far less sure of his position. *The gods will decide his fate. That's not my part.*

The idea of a witch being able to cast a physical place adrift in time boggled Ridge. The power required would be immense, and the skill and knowledge almost unfathomable.

"You said that the old king's witch died. How can you be certain?" Henri asked, and from his expression, Ridge could tell that he'd been just as deeply engrossed in the story.

"We heard reports. As for being certain—it had been long enough ago since we crossed paths that I did not make inquiries. We never heard from him again."

"Do you know anything about how the king's witch 'hid' this place or where the monks and Toland were sent?" Ridge asked.

Brother Sean shook his head. "I didn't ask. I have no magic—what would I make of that knowledge if I had it? The witch did not offer details, and he was fearsome enough that none of us dared to press with questions that didn't matter. Toland was safe. We were spared ruin. It was more than we could have hoped."

Something in his tone made Ridge's attention linger on the old priest's face, taking note of a worried expression. "There's something you're not telling us," Ridge guessed.

"It's probably nothing."

"It might be something."

Brother Sean sighed. "When we first returned to the chapter house, I thought of Toland often and wondered how he was doing, what he looked like as he grew, whether he was happy and well-cared for. As the years went by, I never forgot him, but the memories of that time faded and seemed almost unreal. It was, after all, a long time ago," he added with a self-conscious half-smile.

"Then just this month—more than once—strange dreams troubled my sleep. I dreamed of monks I don't know in a monastery I don't recognize. I can tell that something is wrong. They're worried about something. In my dream, one of the youngest monks looks right at me, and I can see the fear in his eyes. Familiar eyes. That's when I wake up."

Brother Sean shivered. "I can't stop thinking about his eyes. They remind me of Toland. But I don't know how to help—or if he really is that child all grown up."

Ridge had a gnawing suspicion, but he didn't want to speak without first talking to Malachi. "The kingdom is in turmoil after Kristoph's death. These are worrisome times. Perhaps, given that, it's not surprising to have strange dreams."

Brother Sean let out a long breath. "That's what I try to tell myself. But I can't shake the feeling that perhaps I'm lying."

"Thank you for speaking with us," Ridge said. "We won't trouble you again."

Brother Sean's expression reflected sadness instead of his initial anger. "I knew that someday questions would be asked. I can't fix the harm I did. But I have tried to do no further injury, and honor the memory of Calia and Toland in my heart. I'm an old man, hardly in better shape than the ones I care for. If there is a reckoning, I will face it soon."

Ridge and Henri walked in silence back to their horses. Kane met them there.

"I checked the grounds and perimeter and then eavesdropped by the window, so I heard a lot," Kane said. "But even after being with Malachi for years, I've never heard of that sort of magic before. I'm curious to see what Malachi thinks about it."

"If the old king's witch could 'hide' the monk's house somewhere outside of time, then he probably made a place like that to hide Toland—only it's lasted for years," Ridge replied.

Henri nodded, and from his lack of surprise, Ridge figured that he'd come to the same conclusion.

"Just when Rett's broken magic takes him to a monastery that doesn't exist, filled with books on all kinds of forbidden magic—and a monk who says he was taken in as a foundling," Henri added.

Ridge turned to look at Henri. "Are you thinking what I'm thinking?"

Henri snorted as if the answer was obvious. "That somehow, Rett dream walked to where the witch hid Kristoph's bastard? That 'Tom' is really Toland? Seems likely, don't you think?"

"Yeah, it does. We've sort of known where the missing heir was all along—but not how to bring him back. If an obvious solution existed, Malachi would have seen it by now," Ridge said.

"We might not have a lot of time to figure it out," Kane said. "Brother Sean's nightmares worry me. It sounds like the magic might be weakening. We don't know whether the old king's witch meant for Toland and the guardian monks to stay in the hidden place for their entire lives or just until it was safe to bring them home."

Ridge nodded. "Maybe. But Renvar is dead. Kristoph's been king for a while now. Why wait?"

"Maybe the old witch hoped Kristoph would have sired a legitimate heir and secured the succession. Then Toland and the monks could be brought back with no threat to the crown. Toland never needed to know, and the monks—if they knew—could maintain the fiction," Kane suggested.

"What went wrong?" Henri asked. "The witch died. Did that weaken the spell? Or did Makary somehow find out and decide to make sure there were no rivals for whatever puppet he wants to have the Regency Council approve?"

Ridge shrugged. "I don't know. But if the haven the witch created is in danger, we need to figure it out soon—or we could lose Kristoph's true heir."

"If we could shore up the magic somehow, Toland is safer there than here, with the Witch Lord and Noxx on the loose," Kane pointed out. "I'd hate to pull off a desperate rescue just to get him assassinated by one of Makary's crazy followers."

"Shit. You're right," Ridge muttered. "Do you think Malachi knows about this kind of magic?"

Kane grimaced. "Doubtful. I get the impression that 'magic' as a concept is a lot more than any one person can ever master. Malachi's focus has been on power related to his abilities. If the old king's witch had different gifts—he might have studied completely different spells and rituals."

Ridge and Rett had always considered their Sight to be powerful and dangerous. Now that he had gotten to know Malachi, Ridge realized that their ability to sense tainted souls, while useful, paled in comparison to the power wielded by a true witch.

"If Gil can find out more about the witch, maybe Malachi can summon Runcian's ghost even if we can't figure out yet what's bound Kristoph's spirit," Ridge replied. "I have to admit, the meeting with Brother Sean didn't go the way I expected."

"If he was telling the truth, that's a hard burden of guilt to carry all these years," Henri said. "And he truly seemed to care about Toland."

"Which is why I can't shake the feeling that's who the young monk is in Brother Sean's dreams," Ridge said. "It would make sense. I don't think he'd invent someone he'd never met. Maybe because of his emotional connection to Toland, he unconsciously makes a link to wherever Green Knoll is."

Kane nodded. "But because Brother Sean doesn't have Rett's abilities, the link is a lot weaker. He can get a glimpse but not interact. If Toland seemed to be speaking to him, was he somehow aware of Brother Sean's presence?"

Ridge shook his head. "I don't know how Malachi deals with this stuff. Just thinking about everything is giving me a headache."

After they had ridden for a candlemark, Ridge's stomach growled. Breakfast had been a while ago, and since there had been no food offered at the cloister house, his hunger reminded him that they were well past lunch. They had taken a different route home from how they had arrived, just in case they were noticed. Ridge had no intention of leading Makary's men or the rogue Shadows to the elderly monks.

Just as he was about to suggest that they stop long enough to retrieve the hard cheese, bread, and fruit packed in their saddlebags, Ridge saw the Thistledown Inn up ahead. It sat near an unremarkable crossroad, and from its down-at-the-heels appearance, this wasn't a busy trade route.

"What do you think?" he asked the others. "We could stop in long enough for a pint and a sausage egg while we get caught up on the latest news and then we can be on our way pretty quickly." He paused. "And besides, they've got a watering trough and nice grass—the horses could use a break."

Kane eyed the other horses tied up in the front. Ridge knew their companion was looking for the sleek, fast mounts favored by guards, a warning sign. The nags at the inn looked like they had pulled a plow earlier in the day, suggesting that farmers—not warriors—were the pub's customers.

"Make it quick," Kane growled. "Order some for me, but bring it out when you come. I'll keep watch."

Ridge understood Kane's concerns, but at the same time, their ability to get news and gossip was severely curtailed by being guests in Malachi's "prison" tower. He itched to relive the casual evenings spent playing darts and sipping ale at a roadside pub during their journeys, where they heard tidbits that rarely reached official channels.

"If we walk in separately, we'll hear twice as much," Henri said after they had watered the horses and tied them where they could graze.

Ridge nodded. "That works. Stay in sight. Not that we couldn't handle a local cutpurse, but I'd rather not draw attention."

Henri's genius lay in being underestimated. In private, he fairly glowed with wit and personality, but he could snuff out that spark in a heartbeat and make himself utterly ordinary and forgettable—the better to be ignored. Once he blended into the crowd, people spoke freely, forgetting they had a stranger in their midst.

Ridge couldn't help smiling fondly. He often suspected that Henri might be the most talented spy among the three of them.

After a few minutes, Ridge sauntered in. The hard-worn pub catered to farmers and peddlers, from the look of the tired men at the bar and sitting at the tables. Beneath the aroma of roasted onions and boiled potatoes hung a whiff of barn smells and the scent of fresh dirt.

Henri had already made himself at home at the bar, chatting and joking with the men ensconced on either side of him as he waited for his food. Ridge glanced at the barkeeper, who gestured vaguely toward the tables, and picked a spot where he could sit with his back to the wall but close enough to the occupied tables to overhear conversations.

Few people paid attention to their entrance, and those who did quickly returned their focus to their food and companions.

When a serving girl came to take his order, Ridge asked for two sausage eggs and a jug of ale, emphasizing that he had a long way to go and needed to get back on the road. While she went to fetch his meal, Ridge decided to step out back to the latrine and saw Henri's barely perceptible nod of acknowledgment.

He had just stepped up to the trench and started to do business when he felt the point of a knife in his ribs.

"It's bad form to rob a man when he's got his prick in his hand, taking a piss. Not very sporting."

"Didn't expect to see you here, Breckenridge. But the bounty's still good, so I guess this is my lucky day."

Ridge tried to identify the voice. The person knew his name, which meant he was probably a Shadow. He and Rett spent as little time as possible with the other assassins since proximity only led to sniping.

"Conroy." Ridge finally placed the voice, picturing the short, skinny man. "What brings you out here, to the middle of nowhere?"

"Was gonna ask you the same. I'm amazed you're still alive without your partner."

Ridge remembered Conroy as someone who enjoyed provoking a fight and refused to give him that satisfaction.

"Had an errand to run," Ridge lied. "Needed to pick up flour at the mill and milk at the farm. Exciting stuff."

The knife jabbed hard enough for the tip to poke through his clothing. "Try again."

Before Ridge could answer, Conroy suddenly cried out in pain, and the blade drew back. Ridge saw one of Henri's throwing knives lodged in the man's shoulder. That was all the opening Ridge needed to kick hard at his attacker's knee, pivot, and grab Conroy's arm, tossing him into the latrine trench.

Henri stepped up beside Ridge. "Saw you go out, figured you were taking too long. Got your eggs and ale," he said, holding a tied-off piece of cloth aloft, "and saved your nuts," he ended with a smirk.

Conroy stood and unsuccessfully tried to shake off the foul-smelling muck. He glowered at Ridge and Henri, but when he moved to climb out, the sight of the knife in Ridge's hand stopped him where he stood.

"Let him go." A new voice sounded from behind them, and Ridge turned just enough to see another old comrade holding a bow with an arrow nocked and aimed at them.

Ridge sheathed his knife, and Henri slipped his dagger back beneath the sleeve of his coat.

"Now, step away from the ditch. Then we're going to the barn to have a little chat," the archer said as Ridge tried to dredge up the Shadow's name from his memory. *Benson.* "The bounty is good whether you're dead or alive, but personally, I've got a few questions, and I want the satisfaction of making you scream and beg before I kill you."

Benson suddenly stiffened, then fell forward with a throwing knife hilt-deep in his back.

"We all want things we can't have," Kane observed, flicking his gaze from the man on the ground to glare at Conroy in challenge.

"You killed one of the King's Shadows!" Conroy yelped.

"You were going to kill me," Ridge protested.

"And Kristoph's dead, so you don't work for the king anymore. You're just another outlaw," Henri added.

Conroy stood knee-deep in piss and mud. "Going to finish me too?"

"Not worth having to clean the blade," Ridge muttered. "Benson might not be completely dead yet if you get him to a healer." He paused. "I have a message for you to take to Burke."

"Who says I know where Burke is?"

"I put the knife into your friend's lung, not his heart, but if you play games long enough, he'll bleed out anyhow," Kane said in a bored tone.

"Tell Burke that we found what Makary was using to blackmail the regency council candidates. Together with the witnesses you're hiding, that should persuade an honest council of nobles."

"Why should I tell him anything for you?"

Ridge remembered that Conroy had always struck him as hot-headed and not particularly smart. "Because it's the only reason we have for letting you live. Would you like us to reconsider?"

"All right. I'll do it." Conroy looked at the muck-covered ditch and then to his bleeding companion. "How am I supposed to get out of this hole and take him anywhere when I'm covered in shit?"

"Not our problem," Ridge said. "The stink on your outside finally matches your insides."

Ridge and Henri headed for the horses. Kane lingered behind, keeping a wary watch on Conroy, and finally jogged to catch up with them.

"Told you that looking for Burke was a bad idea," he said as they swung up to the saddle and rode away.

"Yeah, you did. Conroy's probably not the only one left with a grudge," Ridge admitted.

Henri rode up between them, still carrying a cloth sack and a jug of ale, which he held aloft with a triumphant grin. "Lucky for you, I grabbed the food before I came out to see why it was taking you so long to piss. Sausage eggs and ale for all of us!"

CHAPTER NINE

R ett tossed and turned as the dream overtook him. Sweat poured down his body, then chills shook him to the bone. He thrashed, kicking his way clear of the bonds that held him.

He smelled the hated flying ointment, the vile mixture that stripped away reality and made nightmares come true.

Rett tried to get away, but his bonds held him in place. Fire burned through his veins one moment and ice the next. His head throbbed, and if he dared open his eyes, he knew he could not trust his vision. Colors bloomed too bright, light pierced his brain, and sounds threatened to make his skull explode.

His muscles bunched, sending tremors of pain down every limb. It felt as if his bones might snap as tendons tightened until his joints were aflame with the slightest movement. Rett's jaw clenched until he thought teeth would break as the cords in his neck strained like they might snap.

His captors had asked no questions and coerced no confessions. Rett understood when they roused him after his last beating that the hallucinations the ointment produced served no purpose beyond pain and humiliation. He had no idea what he said or how he cried out when the mixture turned his blood to quicksilver. No doubt his screams pleased and amused his tormentors.

Rett no longer cared.

He had no anchor, no purpose. King Kristoph was dead. Ridge and Henri, dead as well. No one was coming to save him, and so far, despite Rett's desperate wishes, his torturers refused him the respite of death. Each time they dosed him, Rett prayed that they would mistake the amount, push his battered body past its limits until his heart failed. He wished for death, but the gods no longer listened.

Between one breath and the next, everything changed.

Rett collapsed against a cold stone floor. Bonds no longer held him fast, and the horrifying dreams were gone. He lay still, listening to his pounding heart as he panted for breath and felt the adrenaline gradually fade from his veins.

His sweat-soaked shirt clung to his back, and the stone beneath him leeched the heat from his body. Rett dared to open his eyes and did not recognize the room.

Not the cell where Letwick kept me. Not Rune Keep. None of our apartments. Am I somehow at Green Knoll again?

A door opened, and Rett squeezed his eyes tightly shut against the lamplight. He heard quick footsteps, then knees hitting the floor beside him.

"Rett? Are you awake? Gods—how did you get here?" Brother Tom sounded scared.

"Don't know."

"I found you here in the storage room half a candlemark ago," Tom went on. "You were unconscious, and it sounded like you were in pain. You had a fit, and I was afraid you'd hurt yourself. So I brought you tea and waited for you to wake."

"Thank you," Rett replied, still groggy.

"You surprised me. I didn't expect to see you again. But ... with everything that's going on, I'm glad you're here."

When Rett's brain felt less scrambled, he would try to make sense of what Tom said. At the moment, he focused on slowing his rapid pulse and taking in enough air to keep from panicking.

"Drink this." Tom helped Rett sit and held a cup of fragrant tea to his lips. He took a deep breath, held the flavor in his mouth, let the liquid warm him, and ground himself in his body.

Except, if this is Green Knoll, I'm not physically here. Is my body back at Rune Keep? Am I still alive?

"Thank you." Rett's throat felt like he had swallowed gravel.

"I think the monastery is haunted," Brother Tom blurted.

Rett forced himself to pay attention. "Haunted? Is this new?"

The monk shivered. "I've had this feeling lately like I'm being watched. Only there's no one around. Several times when I felt that, I've gotten up and looked all around, but I'm alone. I thought it was just my imagination, but when it kept happening, I wondered."

"Did anything else occur?" The alarm Rett felt helped him push past his vertigo and queasy stomach.

"I had a dream about a man who was chasing me through the hallways. I dreamed it three times." He dropped his voice. "Sometimes things I dream come true."

The importance of that comment hit Rett, but he filed it away to consider later. *Was Tom left at the monastery because someone feared he might be psychic—like Sofen? Are any of the other monks able to tap into magic? Is that why there's a huge occult library hidden in a cloister that doesn't really exist?*

"Do you know why he was chasing you?"

Tom shook his head. "No ... I just had a bad feeling, and I ran." He hesitated. "Rett, he stared right at me, and he wasn't surprised. It was like he expected to see me."

A chill went down Rett's spine that had nothing to do with his vision. "What did he look like?"

"Sandy hair, pointed nose. Middle years or so, I'd guess. But Rett—if you'd seen his eyes, you'd know why I ran. He was so … cold—like he was a hunter—and I was the prey."

"That's not good," Rett said. *Tom is a monk. He's been in a cloister all his life. I'm an assassin. Even broken, I've got the skills to protect him. There's some reason I keep coming back here. Maybe protecting him—and the other monks—is what I'm meant to do.*

"I was a soldier," Rett told him, figuring that the whole truth might not go over well. "Maybe I can help."

"Let's go to my room. We can talk privately there and not have to sit on the floor." Brother Tom stood and offered him a hand.

Rett followed his host down a corridor until they stopped in front of a door. "It's not very big, but it's home," Tom said with a self-conscious smile. "And I might not have made my bed this morning."

"I've seen worse, believe me."

Rett was still trying to wrap his mind around how he'd gone from his room at Rune Keep to Green Knoll.

Ridge had gone with Kane and Henri to confront the old priest who took Calia's baby. Much as Rett had ached for the ghost when she told her story, and no matter how much he wanted to see her loss avenged, he knew it was better for him to remain with Malachi. Now he wondered if that decision had been prescient.

Brother Tom bustled around, pulling up the blanket on his bed and pushing books and parchment out of the way. "Please, have a seat," he offered, gesturing toward his desk chair while he sat on the edge of his bed.

"Are you the only one who had dreams—or thought there might be a ghost?" Rett asked, ignoring the aftereffects of his fit because intuition warned him that this was too important to overlook.

"No. Brother Kendrick said he had a strange feeling lately as well."

Rett frowned. "What do you know about Kendrick?" Rett asked.

Tom's eyes widened. "Why?"

"Me being here is an accident—I think. You said you were a small child when you came to the monastery. We don't know anything about your past. But Kendrick had a life before Green Knoll—and that might matter. Especially if both of you have had a bad feeling lately, there could be a good reason," Rett said, thinking aloud.

"Brother Kendrick is the oldest. No one says much about their life before, but we've lived together for a long time, so little pieces add up. Some of the monks had lived in other cloisters. A few had a regular life and then made a big change—usually, after they lost someone," Tom said. "One or two had wives, families, farms. Something went wrong. People died. They sought a fresh start, a vocation—"

"A calling," Rett said, and Brother Tom nodded.

"Exactly."

Rett would never be able to explain that he felt the same way about his own vastly different job.

"And everyone who had been somewhere else has said that they never felt like they fit in—until Green Knoll."

Rett's suspicions grew even stronger at Tom's words. A cloister that no one had ever heard of, full of misfit monks and jam-packed with grimoires and magical books, seemed like far too much of a coincidence.

Did they get exiled or sent into an elaborate hiding place to protect them? Who sent them here, and why? The priests and the army have been the only ones allowed to have magic for quite a while. These are all monks, so why would it matter?

Brother Tom rose and paced. "Strange things have been happening. The ground shakes. We've had unusually bad storms. People and animals have gotten hurt, and buildings have been damaged. Sometimes, I'm afraid it might be the end of the world."

Rett's heart pounded at the words, even though he knew Tom probably didn't mean them literally. *If there's something magical about this place and someone created it, then maybe someone else can unmake it. The Witch Lord? Why would he care—unless he wants something that he thinks is in the hidden library.*

The tolling of a bell broke the cloister's silence. Brother Tom looked stricken. "Something's wrong. That one only rings in emergencies." He headed for the door, and Rett got up to follow.

"You've got to stay here," Brother Tom begged. "Someone might see you."

Rett met his gaze. "I think that maybe I was sent here to protect you. I need to be with you to do that. I can stay out of sight—but I want to be close." He could see the internal debate in Tom's face before the monk finally nodded.

"All right. But try not to get caught."

Rett couldn't help grinning in response. "That's sort of a specialty of mine. I'll do my best."

A few moments' delay in responding to the alarm meant they were alone in the corridors, and Tom was the last to arrive. Rett found a vantage point where he could see without being easily seen.

He recognized Kendrick from the prior visit when the stern monk had caught him in the library. Now, the older man looked grief-stricken, aged by worry.

"Brother Harris is dead," Kendrick announced, and the others gasped or cried out in shock.

"How did he die?" One of the monks asked. "We just saw him at breakfast."

"Where did he die?" another asked.

Kendrick hesitated before speaking. "We aren't entirely sure of the circumstances yet, but Brother Warren and I are looking into the matter. Until we know more, I don't want anyone to leave the building alone—that includes going to the garden or the barn."

The whispers among the group and their expressions of alarm suggested to Rett that whatever had befallen Harris, the other monks were unlikely suspects.

I'm here, and I shouldn't be. Could someone else have gotten in as well? But who—and why?

"Brother Warren and I will be speaking with each of you to try to figure out what happened and if you might have seen something. Please don't discuss the matter until then, and don't withhold any detail, no matter how small or seemingly unimportant. Thank you—and be extra careful," Kendrick added.

The group dispersed, and amid the whispers, Rett could sense how the mood had shifted from curiosity to worry—and fear. *I'd wager that nothing much surprising ever happens here. If Harris's death was unremarkable, there wouldn't be an investigation, and he would have named the cause.*

Could it be suicide? Rett considered. *Maybe—but I think Kendrick would have couched his wording differently in that case. It's too late now to bother finding out if Harris was troubled or unhappy. If he didn't die of natural causes and he didn't kill himself, then there's some reason for Kendrick to suspect murder.*

But did one of the monks kill Harris, or was it the "haunt" that Tom sensed?

Rett watched Tom linger to speak with Kendrick, and after a brief conversation, come away looking confused and disturbed. When he caught up with Tom in the corridor, the monk gave a quick shake of his head to indicate not wanting to speak about the incident until they were behind closed doors.

"Do people die often?" Rett asked once they retreated to Tom's room.

Tom walked over to the washbasin to splash his face with water, and even at a distance, Rett could see how the man's hands shook.

"No. I've lived almost my whole life here." Tom paced again as Rett sat in the chair, out of the way. "There's only been one other death that I can remember, and he was very old. We grieved his loss, but no one questioned the circumstances or thought anything amiss."

"How far back can you remember?"

Tom thought for a moment. "Twenty-five years? I'm twenty-seven."

"One death before this in that long? That seems unusually lucky."

Tom shrugged. "We have good food, plenty of exercise and fresh air, and a peaceful community."

Rett wasn't sure how his next query would be received. "Tom, do any of the monks have special abilities?"

Tom looked confused. "A few are very talented musicians, several of them cook well, and Brother Harris was particularly good at woodworking. Is that what you mean?"

Rett shook his head. "I don't mean talents or skills. Do the others dream about things that come true or speak to ghosts or know things that no one's told them?" He didn't miss the glint of fear in Tom's eyes.

"You mean magic."

"Magic wasn't forbidden when Renvar was king. Why does it frighten you to talk about it?"

Tom startled. "*Was* king?"

Rett cursed himself for accidentally taking the conversation off track in what might be a dangerous direction. "His son, Kristoph, has been king for a while now." He smiled to cover his mistake. "Since you don't get news from outside, of course you wouldn't know."

"Sometimes it's hard to believe there's anything beyond the walls. But you came from there, so it must be real." Tom looked hard at Rett. "What aren't you telling me?"

So many things I don't even know where to begin.

"I suspect that the cloister is under some kind of protection spell," Rett said. "Maybe to keep all those rare books and manuscripts safe or out of the wrong hands. If these monks came together to protect the library, and they weren't going to have contact with the outside world, then bringing a child with them makes sense—they'd need a range of ages so people could carry on for as long as possible."

"What about the haunting? Do you think the ghost hurt Brother Harris?" Tom looked aghast, and Rett remembered how sheltered the monk was.

"I think that's a mystery that needs to be solved," Rett said. "Do you want to investigate it with me?"

Tom looked hesitant. "Isn't that what Kendrick and Warren are doing? They're the senior monks."

Rett shrugged. "Maybe we could look closely all around the cloister and see if anything's been damaged or disturbed, like it might be if someone else is here who shouldn't be—besides me. And we might find some clues in the library if you'll show me around again."

"All right. I can't see how that would get in Kendrick's way," Tom replied. "We'd actually be helping him by getting more done in less time."

"Exactly."

Tom's eyes narrowed and Rett wondered what the other man was thinking. "We need to make sure no one sees you," Tom said finally. "I don't want them taking the easy answer to Harris's death and figuring you for the killer, since you're a stranger to them."

"I agree. But remember what I said about having been a soldier. I'm pretty good at not getting caught."

They waited until the middle of the night when the other monks were asleep and the monastery was quiet. Rett and Tom slipped silently down the corridor, away from the sleeping areas. Rett wasn't sure what they were looking for; after all, his random appearances didn't leave any evidence behind.

Then again, I didn't magic myself here—at least not intentionally. My abilities aren't stable after what Letwick did to me, and when I have a fit, that seems to make strange things happen and sends me here.

It would be awfully damn unusual for someone else to get here for the same reasons. So that means whoever is "haunting" the cloister had to find another way to get in. And assuming they don't mean to stay, they need to have a way home and maybe a place to hide. If we can find that, we might find them.

Rett and Tom avoided the common areas since they were well-trafficked enough that someone would have noticed anything strange. All of the sleeping rooms were occupied except for two, and Tom volunteered to check those before going to breakfast in the morning.

That left them with storage rooms like the one where Tom had found Rett, as well as the barns and outbuildings.

"We have dogs and chickens," Tom had said when Rett suggested starting outside. "They make a racket when anyone comes near. If we went there now, we'd wake everyone before we even reached the fence. We take turns working in the garden and caring for the animals, and it's a dawn-to-dusk job. So if someone showed up and left behind evidence, it would have been noticed."

"Unless Harris did—and that's what got him killed," Rett replied.

"I guess that's possible," Tom agreed. "Let's visit the storage rooms and then the library. I'll bring you something to eat before I start my chores, and if we take some of the books back to my room, you can research all day while I'm managing my chores. Maybe you'll find something, or perhaps I'll hear about someone else having a strange experience."

"It shouldn't take long for Kendrick and Harris to talk to all the monks. There aren't many to interview."

"Depends on how long a conversation they have with each one, but they should still be finished by suppertime, I'd think," Tom said.

The storage rooms showed no indication that anything was amiss or that anyone had been working rituals or hiding there. Rett itched to figure out what was going on, sure that the "haunted" feeling Tom and Kendrick reported was linked somehow to the monk's death—and perhaps, even more danger.

As they neared the library, Tom froze and signaled for Rett to halt and be quiet. Rett's eyes widened as he heard quick footsteps not far ahead of them, but when they turned the corner, no one was in sight.

"I've got that haunted feeling again, like someone can see us, but we can't see them," Tom whispered. Rett felt even more sure than before that Tom possessed some kind of prescience. If they lived through this adventure, that was something they needed to discuss.

"I heard someone too. And if they're not a ghost, they've got to be in the library," Rett murmured. He wished that his weapons had materialized here with him, but they hadn't. All he had for protection was a large butcher knife he grabbed from a storage room, despite Tom's look of utter horror. Rett had the knife in hand as they opened the door, ready for an ambush.

The dark, deserted library had an eerie feel. Rett and Tom slipped inside, and Tom opened the shutters on his lantern. The glow of his single candle left most of the cavernous area deep in shadow, raising the hair on the back of Rett's neck as he realized how vulnerable they were if an attacker lay in wait in the dark.

"Will you get in trouble for being here if we get caught?" Rett whispered.

"I wouldn't be the first one who couldn't sleep and came to the library. But I'd have some explaining to do about you."

They lit a second lantern from a table inside the doorway and moved cautiously amid the cavernous rows of tall bookshelves that receded into blackness.

"This is insane," Rett muttered. "We're sitting ducks."

They moved slowly, checking each row as they went, with Rett on the right and Tom on the left. *If someone else ran in here before us, they can't have gotten too far. They're either going to try to let us pass and run out behind us or seize the advantage.*

Rett pivoted on instinct as one of the shadows moved. He sensed magic rising, directed at Tom, not at him. Before he could shout a warning, Rett threw himself in front of Tom. He stabbed with the kitchen knife, aiming for the heart, but the man twisted at the last second, and Rett slipped the blade between ribs to hit a lung instead. Then he called up *something* from deep inside—pure self-preservation.

Tom gasped as Rett grabbed the intruder and held on tight. His only plan in that moment was to stop the stranger from killing Tom.

"What are you?" The man hissed. Strange magic sparked along Rett's skin, but he held on, knowing that if the attacker got a second chance, Rett wouldn't be able to keep Tom from being hurt.

"Here to stop you." The tingle turned hot, fire dancing through his veins. Rett doubted he could win a battle arcane against a true mage. *Unless I cheat.*

Gritting his teeth against the pain, Rett focused on going home. He pictured the room at Rune Keep, visualizing every detail, willing himself to go back. At the same time, Rett *pulled*, drawing on his own rogue magic and in a moment of desperation, reaching out to grab from their attacker as well.

He imagined holding a fistful of lightning, and then he *shoved* with all his might. Rett expected to find himself tumbling through dreams and nightmares to wake in his own bed, like always before, perhaps with the stranger in a heap on the floor.

Currents of invisible power rushed around them, pulling at their essence instead of their bodies. Rett dug in his fingers, intending to push the attacker into that riptide even at the cost of burning himself up. He was at the center of a maelstrom and feared that he and his assailant might be swept away together.

A hand closed around Rett's left ankle, painfully tight.

"I've got you," Tom shouted. "And I won't let go."

Rett brought his arms up, breaking the attacker's hold, and pushed him away, then kicked with all his might with his free leg. That ripped him loose from the stranger's grip and sent the man flailing backward into the storm that swallowed him whole.

The attacker and the vortex disappeared. Rett didn't.

He lay on the library floor, stunned that he was still at the cloister, and wondering what in the name of the gods had just happened.

"Rett?" Tom squawked, sounding panicked.

"He's gone." Rett couldn't explain why he remained and the attacker hadn't, but he knew for certain that the other man was no longer in the cloister. "I ... sent him away."

"There was a flash of light, and I saw his face. That was the man from my dreams, the one who was chasing me." Even in the lantern's glow, Tom looked pale and shaken.

"He wasn't after me. He was looking for you," Rett said, switching into battle mode, locking away his emotions and shifting into cold logic. The pieces fell into place, and while he didn't have proof, it would explain a lot.

"Me? I'm nobody."

"Apparently that's not true," Rett said, climbing to his feet.

The library door slammed open, and the light from a large lantern nearly blinded them. Tom dodged in front of Rett, throwing his arms wide protectively.

"Who are you?"

Rett saw Brother Kendrick in the doorway, backed by several other monks. Kendrick had a black eye, and blood seeped from a split eyebrow.

"He saved me," Tom interjected, staying between Kendrick and Rett, protecting his defender with his own body.

"Move out of the way, Tom," Kendrick ordered.

"The man—the one I saw in my dream—he was here. The one *you said* you saw in yours," Tom blurted. "Rett saved me."

"Someone sent an assassin to kill Tom—and apparently, you." Rett met Kendrick's gaze and saw the other flinch. "And I think you know why."

"Brother Kendrick?" Tom's voice had lost its defiance and sounded pleading. "What's going on?"

Kendrick looked from Rett to Tom, then turned to the monks behind him. "Search the cloister top to bottom—including the farm. Stay in pairs or triads. No one goes anywhere alone. Go armed—and do whatever you must to capture the intruder."

"He's not here. I sent him back," Rett said, and the others stared at him. "He used magic to get here—I used it to make him leave. I want to know why something keeps dragging me here and why the magic that holds this place together is starting to fail."

Kendrick stared at Rett with a combination of suspicion and disbelief. He turned back to the other monks. "Go. Rally the others. When you're finished, go to the dining hall." His companions left, and Kendrick glanced between Rett and Tom.

"Come to the office. Sounds like we've both got a lot of questions."

Kendrick's office had the same sparse furnishings as the rest of the monastery—solid, functional pieces without fuss or ornamentation. The rough plaster-over-rock walls were plain white, except for one painted with a mural of a sunset.

Kendrick settled behind his desk while Rett and Tom sat in the chairs facing him. He turned to Rett once more. "Who are you, and why are you here?"

"I was a soldier," Rett replied, sticking to his story. Bringing up the Shadows would complicate things and raise doubts. *Besides, technically I'm not a Shadow anymore.*

"I was on guard duty with King Kristoph when there was an explosion. It killed the king and a lot of other people. I almost died. One of the people behind the bombing tortured me. I'd always had a bit of magic before, but what they did somehow expanded my abilities. Sometimes, I have fits, and that's when I've shown up here." Rett paused. "Everyone here has a bit—or more than a bit—of magic, don't they?"

Kendrick's startled look before he got hold of himself gave Rett his answer. "The king's witch sent us here to protect the arcane library," he finally replied. "We all came willingly. Tom was very young. The king had started to distrust magic and witches, and Runcian feared the worst. He didn't want the lore to be destroyed."

Rett nodded. "I believe you—but that's only part of the story." He looked at Tom, whose guileless, wide-eyed expression dispelled any questions Rett had as to whether or not the young man suspected.

"The biggest reason was to hide him," Rett said with a sad smile.

"I don't know what—" Tom protested.

"You are the most important person in the whole kingdom right now," Rett said. "Your name is Toland. Your mother was Calia. And your father was a teenager who grew up to be king.

Kristoph died without a legitimate heir. That makes you the next king of Landria."

Kendrick had gone so pale Rett thought the man might faint. Tom's mouth opened and closed like a beached fish for a few seconds in utter shock before he turned to stare at his mentor. "Is that true?"

All Kendrick could manage was a nod.

"There's a man—Yefim Makary, his followers call him the Witch Lord. He was behind several prior attempts on King Kristoph's life, and he masterminded the attack that killed the king—and almost killed me. I believe he sent the assassin who killed Brother Harris and attacked you and Tom," Rett said, looking at the purple bruises and crusted blood on Kendrick's face.

"No one knew we were here," Kendrick said, his voice a broken whisper. "Only the king's witch and the priest who took Toland from his mother."

"Someone obviously found out," Rett replied. "Makary's supporters will kill and torture anyone to find out what they want to know. And those tremors and strange omens—you know what they are, don't you?"

"Yes," Kendrick said, looking sick. "Someone is trying to break the magic that sustains this place. It was never meant to be undone." He looked at Tom. "We needed to keep you safe, keep you from being everyone's pawn. We came here willingly, expecting to live out our lives and die of old age."

"My whole life has been a lie?" Tom sounded stunned, but Rett knew that before long, anger would replace the shock.

"I'm sorry that we did not tell you," Kendrick said. "We had one chaotic night to save your life. Kristoph's father ordered your death. He didn't think you would be a 'suitable' heir for political reasons. If anyone except Brother Sean had been sent to take you that night, you would have died.

"But Sean knew the order was wrong, and so a handful of us defied the king. Then Runcian worked forbidden magic and created Green Knoll to keep you safe. I'm sorry for not telling you the whole truth and that you didn't get a normal upbringing, but I'll never regret saving your life."

Tom still looked poleaxed. "I'm just a monk. I don't know anything about being king."

Kendrick cleared his throat. "That's not completely true. The history project you've been 'helping research' has been part of your education. All the projects, everything you learned—taught you a prince's lessons. We agreed from the start that would be wise, just in case this moment came." He met Tom's gaze with true regret. "I hoped it never would."

Rett's head snapped up. "Wait. If you educated Tom as a prince 'just in case,' then you must have thought the spell that cut Green Knoll off from the world could be undone."

Kendrick shrugged. "Runcian believed that Kristoph would eventually have a legitimate heir and that there would be no reason for us to return. The cloister is self-sufficient. Those of us who volunteered expected to remain permanently."

"Did Runcian create an escape door?" Rett asked.

Kendrick shrugged again. "In a fashion. While it's true that each of us here have a bit of magic, we're not as powerful as the king's witch who created the spell. Runcian told me that he was leaving a copy of the ritual in the library for an emergency but that he didn't expect we would ever have to use it."

"Do you know where?" Rett demanded.

"No. We never went looking for it. There was no reason to do so. Some things are too dangerous to know," Kendrick replied.

"You need to find it. Everything you've done won't matter if we can't leave Green Knoll and the Witch Lord breaks the magic sustaining it," Rett reminded them. "Do you think that's why the intruder attacked you—because he thought you knew the way to reverse the spell?"

"I'm part of the spell," the older monk replied. "So much happened so fast. But Runcian knew me from long ago, and he asked me personally to be the abbot of the cloister. He told me I would be the anchor for the magic, and in turn, the magic would also extend our lives."

"If the Witch Lord found that out, then he probably figures that killing you would weaken the magic—or break it," Rett said.

"I don't think that's true. Runcian couldn't come with us, and he needed a proxy—me." Kendrick looked worried and confused.

"When I threw the assassin out, it should have snapped me back to where I came from. But it didn't. Always before, the connection just faded and I was gone, but it's already been longer than any other visit," Rett said.

He looked from Kendrick to Tom, hoping he kept his fear at bay. "I think I'm stuck here."

Chapter Ten

"How did you lose him—again?" Ridge tried and failed to control his temper.

"He wandered off," Malachi snapped. "I was working on how to crush the garnet and a couple of other spells. I thought he knew better than to try to soul travel without me."

"Rett doesn't always control that." Ridge defended his partner. "Especially not if he takes a fit on the heels of a vision. How long has he been like this?"

Ridge, Kane, and Henri had returned from their mission with a sense of triumph at what they learned from the old priest. After everything they'd been through, it had been pleasant to bask in the glow of a win while it lasted.

That triumph had faded as soon as they returned to Rune Keep and found Rett unconscious, arching and twitching.

"I've been with him for the last candlemark," Malachi replied. "Usually, his visit to the monastery is brief. I thought he was about to return at one point, and then abruptly, he didn't."

"Is he stuck ... really stuck?" Ridge knew that Malachi could hear the worry and fear in his voice.

"I can feel the energy around him, and it's ... wrong."

"Wrong, how?" Ridge's worry rose, concerned that Malachi didn't have a ready answer.

"Like it's been twisted. That might happen if a powerful spell forced itself past a barrier. Rett travels to Green Knoll through a … flaw … that doesn't recognize him as a stranger because his consciousness and not his body crosses the boundary. And because the monks exist somewhere other than our world, he seems solid to them."

Cold dread settled in Ridge's stomach. "Do you think Noxx—"

Malachi shook his head. "Alone? No. But he and Makary together—or Makary and another witch—might be able to damage the old spell if they knew what they were looking for."

"We can worry about who and why later," Ridge said as a tremor ran through Rett's form. "Right now, we need to bring him back."

"I think I know a way." Malachi plucked a hair from Rett's head, then stood straight. "Stay with him. I have to gather some things I'll need."

Ridge put a hand on Rett's shoulder. "I'm here. Malachi is going to help you find your way. Just don't get lost. We'll bring you home."

Rett's body trembled, and Ridge tightened his grip as if he could will his partner back across the void that separated soul from body.

It'll be all right. It has to be.

Ridge kept hoping, but Rett didn't wake. He told Rett stories of how his day had gone, about what they had seen and heard, just to fill the silence.

Malachi returned after a while with a basin, candles, fragrant spices, and dried plant leaves, things Ridge recognized from other spell work.

"Keep your hold on him. It'll help ground Rett in this world," Malachi told Ridge. "I'm going to build a bridge to guide him back."

"Why does he need a bridge when he's been able to find his way before?"

"The energy of the hidden cloister has changed since he and I visited together. It feels damaged, not as solid as before," Malachi replied.

"What could damage it?" Ridge felt cold fear spread in his chest.

"Magic." Malachi met his gaze. "No spell is strong enough to be completely safe from sabotage if the Witch Lord somehow ferreted out what you just learned from the old priest and had a strong enough mage at his disposal, he could use magic to attack—and weaken—the spell. If he can cause 'cracks' in the protection, he might even be able to send someone inside. Rett proved—accidentally—that such a thing is possible."

"Send someone? Like a thief?" Ridge felt his worry spike again.

"Or an assassin."

"What happens if the spell fails while there are people inside?" Ridge knew he didn't want to hear the answer.

"Nothing good. Which is why we need to figure out how Runcian worked the spell so we can unravel it—safely."

Ridge glared at Malachi. "I thought you were going to summon King Renvar and Runcian."

"What do you think I was trying to do when Rett got lost in his head again?" Malachi snapped. "The spell failed. Renvar's spirit isn't within reach. He's moved on—whether willingly or not, I don't know."

"And Runcian?" Ridge asked.

Malachi shook his head. "If Runcian's ghost remains, he's hidden what's left of himself to protect Toland and Green Knoll. I also wouldn't be surprised if the old witch sacrificed himself to feed the power of the protection spell that keeps the cloister out of reach."

Ridge didn't know a lot about true magic, but anything to do with blood or life energy—or souls—made for powerful spells.

"I have a summoning spell that I've changed to suit the occasion," Malachi said. "I think it will guide Rett back to us. And once we have that taken care of, I've got an idea on how to destroy the garnet anchor stone."

Ridge stayed beside Rett as Malachi prepared a warded circle and lit the candles. The mage spoke quietly as he added one ingredient after another into the bowl, and finally, a single brown hair.

Malachi finished the incantation, and as he called out the final words, a violet flame rose from the bowl, and the candles flickered wildly. Even Ridge felt the energy in the room rise and fall, and it made the hair on his arms stand on end.

Rett twisted and cried out, eyes open but unseeing. Ridge grabbed Rett's shoulders, pinning him just enough to keep him from thrashing and hurting himself.

Just as Ridge opened his mouth to shout for Malachi's help, Rett suddenly fell back against the floor, limp and pale.

"Rett?" Ridge felt his throat tighten, afraid to hope.

Rett groaned, but he did not open his eyes. The tremors were gone, and warmth slowly came back to his skin.

Malachi finished the rest of the ritual, thanking the elements and extinguishing the candles. When he broke the warded circle, he turned and placed his hand on Rett's chest.

"He's back."

Ridge heard the exhaustion in Malachi's voice and knew that the magic had drained him. "Is he all right?"

"As far as I can tell. We'll need to wait until he wakes to know for certain. Being stuck—lost—tired him. He may sleep for quite a while. That would be best."

"I'll sit with him," Ridge said.

Malachi quirked an eyebrow. "You haven't exactly had a quiet day yourself."

Ridge gave a half-shrug. "Maybe I'll nap. He shouldn't be alone."

"I'll have Henri bring food for both of you," Malachi said. "I think we could all use a good meal."

"Did you pick up on anything when you did your spell?" Ridge asked as Malachi walked toward the door to the room.

"I wonder if something is pulling Rett to Green Knoll," Malachi mused. "Maybe it isn't as random as it looks."

"Meaning?" Ridge demanded.

Malachi shook his head. "I'm not sure. Rett's abilities were altered by what Letwick did to him. We don't completely understand the extent of those changes—and neither does he. I've got a theory that maybe a part of him knows that he's needed and sends him."

"Fuck. That's not good. He should be able to choose. It shouldn't be chosen for him."

"No argument. I think right now, it's instinct. Need calls to power or something like that. Rett could probably learn to control it and refuse the pull. But that would take time, training, and study. This is all new—it's going to take a while to figure out."

"You think that because we swore to protect the king, and Kristoph's true heir is in danger, Tom—Toland—somehow called to Rett's magic and sucked him into the cloister?" As much as Ridge hated the lack of control that implied, it made a certain kind of sense.

"Maybe. We're figuring this out as we go. And trying not to lose the kingdom while we're doing it," Malachi replied.

Ridge did his best to keep from fidgeting, especially when he saw tremors race through Rett's unconscious form.

"Noxx might have believed all this time that the priest really did kill Toland—Tom," Malachi corrected himself. "We already know he's been working with Makary for a while. Then somehow, they find out that Toland didn't die. Having the true heir return would cause Makary big problems. He's going to try to prevent that—at any cost."

Ridge frowned. "I didn't have the impression that Makary had much magic of his own, and Noxx doesn't seem powerful enough to create a 'pocket' to hide a whole cloister for more than twenty years."

"Neither of them have that kind of power—on their own," Malachi replied. "Which very well might be why they're stealing the life energy of the people they make into their *kolvry* fighters. Noxx gets revenge on people who've wronged him by working the spell on them, and as a bonus he gains pawns to protect him. Then he and Malachi work bigger spells together than they could alone—like the one to bewitch the regency council members."

"And here's another tidbit," Malachi added. "Gil sent a messenger while you were out. He's been able to trace all of the nominees for a regency council back to that hunting party when Calia and Kristoph were forced together."

"I guess I shouldn't be surprised. Didn't Duke Letwick also have a younger brother? He'd also be a contender for the throne now that the duke is dead," Ridge said.

"Gil's been looking into that. His sources say that Garett Letwick, the brother, booked passage on a ship headed to

Brewynn the day after Kristoph died. His ship, the *Fortitude,* and all on board went down in a storm."

"Convenient," Ridge muttered.

"Two other ships were battling the same storm, and the surviving crews reported they saw lightning strike the *Fortitude* and set the sails on fire right before she was swamped by a wave and capsized," Malachi replied. "No one's seen Garett Letwick since then. I tried to summon his spirit without luck. Either he's moved on, or we've got yet another hidden ghost."

"Or he's not dead," Ridge said stubbornly.

"If he tried to flee the country, it doesn't sound like he wants the crown," Malachi pointed out.

"Unless he's savvy enough to try to line up foreign backing. That way, he could claim the throne without being beholden to Makary," Ridge replied.

"Let's not invent new crises. We haven't finished with the ones we've got," Malachi said.

"Apparently, there's a long line of disloyal lords just waiting for an opportunity."

"Certainly seems that way." He paused. "But on a positive note, Luc said he'd find a way to pick up the blackmail information, and Gil will get it into the hands of people at court. And I think I've figured out how to smash the garnet without killing us all."

"Blackmail, blood magic, murdering monks, and looting monasteries," Ridge muttered. "This gets worse and worse the more we know."

"But Rett is back with us. We haven't had a lot of wins. Take it and be glad," the necromancer said and managed a tired smile as he left the room.

⚜ ⚜ ⚜

Ridge jolted awake as he heard Rett moan and shift in his bed. "Hey there, go easy. You've had a rough time of it," he said, in a voice scratchy with sleep.

"Where am I?" Rett murmured.

"Rune Keep. Malachi brought you home from Green Knoll."

"Need to go back," Rett protested. "They're being attacked."

"We'll figure it out," Ridge promised. "When you've recovered."

Rett shook his head fiercely. "No time. Danger."

"We don't know how to protect them, but Malachi is working on it. You're going to help—so you have to recover. Henri will bring food, and it's my job to make sure you sleep. Malachi and Gil are figuring out how to stop Noxx and find the Witch Lord. Next time you wake up, you can tell us what happened. But for now, get some rest," Ridge instructed.

He could tell that Rett wanted to argue, but exhaustion overcame even his stubborn partner's resistance, and Rett slept.

Henri came to the door candlemarks later. "I have soup and bread for you, with brandy to warm the blood. Go and eat. I'll sit with Rett."

Ridge opened his mouth to protest, but Henri shook his head. "If he wakes, I'll call you. You're just in the other room. Don't make me send the scary witch in here after you."

"I heard that," Malachi said from the other room, followed by Kane's laugh.

"Guess I have to go, or he'll turn you into a toad," Ridge said as he got to his feet.

Henri sat with his back against the wall so he could watch Rett, and Ridge headed to the other room where Malachi and

Kane were waiting for him. A bowl of broth and noodles sat next to a glass with a generous serving of brandy.

"Eat. Restore your strength," Malachi said, with a look that Ridge felt certain saw down to his soul.

The hot soup eased Ridge's sleep-scratchy throat and warmed him. He wondered if Henri was to thank for the excellent flavor or if Malachi's magic had something to do with the way the broth seemed to heal him from within.

When Ridge finished, he sipped the brandy and leaned back, looking at Malachi and Kane. "What you've been teaching Rett about how to use his new magic—can he protect himself? Can he use it to fight beside us? Because I saw what he did at the plague shrine, how harnessing his magic almost killed him. There has to be a better way."

Malachi and Kane exchanged a look, and the necromancer regarded Ridge for a moment before he answered. "When you first learned to be a warrior, were you injured in training?"

"Sure. That's how it works. Pain is a good teacher. It reminds you what not to do again."

Malachi nodded. "Magic isn't so different. Rett's abilities were broken open by what the duke did to him, which is why his progress is different from the gradual growth that usually happens. We're not entirely sure what the torture unlocked or why. It's all uncharted territory."

"You're not making me feel any better." Ridge poured himself another slug of brandy.

"The truth usually doesn't."

"There's more to Gil's last message," Kane said. "Brother Sean and the elderly monks are dead."

Ridge's head snapped up, and his eyes went wide. "What?"

"They were murdered," Malachi answered. "Either Noxx or one of his helpers. Gil says that magic was involved. The chapter house wasn't as defended as Green Knoll, but Runcian hadn't left them wholly unprotected. The grounds were warded. Those monks weren't mages, so they couldn't defend themselves. Someone got past the safeguards."

"Just like you suspect happened at Green Knoll," Ridge said.

Malachi nodded. "Yes. Noxx and the Witch Lord, with their stolen energy, are doing powerful magic. I wonder if they've come upon old texts to find spells like that. Gil also said that bandits—our guess is some of Makary's minions—have been raiding monasteries and stealing from them."

"Then we've got to find our version of how to cross those magical barriers," Ridge said.

"Runcian left his spells in the library at Green Knoll."

They all looked up when Rett spoke from the doorway. He still looked worn and pale, but Ridge knew better than to argue him back to bed.

Henri stood just behind Rett with a resigned look. "He wouldn't stay down, and I didn't think you'd be all right with me bashing him on the head."

"No bashing," Ridge confirmed.

Henri gave a put-upon sigh. "Oh, all right. Fine."

Ridge waved for him to come to the table. "I already ate. The soup is good." Ridge made room for Rett to sit beside him while Henri went to get Rett soup.

"Tell us about what happened when you went visiting," Kane urged.

Ridge poured brandy for Rett, who accepted it gratefully. Ridge and the others waited for Rett to eat, then listened as

Rett recounted the events at the hidden cloister. Even Henri lingered in the doorway to hear the story.

"Kendrick and Tom are looking for Runcian's spell. They may have already found it. If I can go back with Malachi, we can perform the magic to reinforce the wardings and keep Tom and the others safe."

"What about bringing Tom back to be the heir?" Kane asked.

"Until we can stop the Witch Lord, Tom's safer at Green Knoll," Malachi said. "We lose everything if we lose Tom."

Ridge couldn't argue with that logic, but he still didn't like the choices that left them. *Bring Tom back, and he's at risk here. Leave him at Green Knoll, and Makary and Noxx could send a better assassin—or just make the whole place cease to exist.*

"On the bright side, who's in the mood for a bonfire?" Malachi asked with a wicked smile. The others turned to stare at him.

"A bonfire?" Kane echoed, incredulous.

"There's an abandoned mill not too far from here. Got damaged in a flood, and the owner walked away from it. The grinding stones are still there. I can use magic to move them. They're heavy enough to crush the garnet," Malachi laid out his plan. "Then we burn the dust like Noxx told you. Setting the rest of the mill on fire is optional."

Ridge looked at Henri. "I swear you're a bad influence. That sounds like something you'd come up with."

Henri grinned. "Thank you. I'll take that as a compliment."

"When?" Rett asked. His hands had a vise grip on his cup, but Ridge knew the determined look in his partner's eyes.

"The sooner, the better," Kane spoke up. "If we break Makary's hold on the regency council candidates, maybe they'll start squabbling—and when the blackmail information gets released, they'll set on each other like wild dogs to deny they knew about the plot to kill Kristoph."

"And if Makary has to bring his unruly would-be council members in line—or find others—maybe there won't be time for things like having the loyal nobles arrested or Duke Foster's siege of Harrowmont."

"From what Gil's heard from Lorella, Lady Sally Anne's people and the ghosts were holding the attackers at bay, but I'm sure it would be a relief to them for the troops to pack up and leave," Malachi said.

"Maybe by the time all this is over, we'll be rid of the Witch Lord's nobles, and Lady Sally Anne and the others won't have to worry about that kind of thing ever again." Ridge wished with all his heart that might come true, but he knew better than to count on it.

Compared to the drama of finding Makary's garnet, getting rid of it wasn't nearly the spectacle Ridge envisioned. Since Malachi had to be present, they left in the middle of the night.

Rett and Henri stayed behind at Rune Keep, and for once Rett didn't protest—giving Ridge a clear idea that his partner hadn't recovered from his latest trip to Green Knoll.

"Looks like the mill is still standing—for now," Kane said as they drew up in front of the dilapidated structure. Flooding had damaged the waterwheel and the roof was storm-battered. The whole structure leaned to one side, making Ridge wonder if it might come down on their heads. The elements weathered the wooden siding a ghostly gray.

Malachi led the way, carrying a lantern in one hand and a sack with the garnet chunk in the other.

The inside of the mill was as decrepit as Ridge feared. Dust, leaves, and spiderwebs covered every surface, making it clear no one had been here in a long while.

"Millstones are still in place. That's all we need," Kane noted. Ridge moved to take the lantern and hold it aloft while Kane and Malachi set out the garnet where it could be crushed between the two heavy stones.

Malachi turned to Kane and Ridge. "I'll use magic to move the millstones. I think I can hold a protective barrier between us and the mill, in case crushing the garnet is a little more … exciting, than it should be."

"Meaning, it explodes?" Kane asked in a dry voice.

"It could happen," Malachi admitted. "If we can collect the dust and burn it in the bowl I brought in my saddlebags, that's preferred. Otherwise, I'll sprinkle the other ritual elements over what's left of the mill and set the place on fire."

"You *really* have been spending too much time with Henri," Ridge muttered.

They retreated from the mill and made sure the horses were tied securely at a safe distance.

"Let's see what happens." Malachi raised one hand and the air between them and the mill took on a faint blue glow. Malachi lifted the other hand and murmured words Ridge couldn't quite catch. The witch's brows furrowed in concentration, and his body tensed. From inside the mill, Ridge heard the scrape and crunch of the old stones moving one last time.

A blinding flare lit up the night as the mill exploded. Ridge and Kane threw their arms up to protect themselves, but Malachi's barrier held against the flying debris. The witch staggered, and Ridge's head rang with the magic behind the blast. Kane instantly moved forward to steady Malachi, who kept his eyes on the collapse of the ramshackle mill.

When the dust settled, the building lay in a heap of splintered wood and chunks of shattered millstone.

"Please tell me that after all that, the garnet actually did get crushed and that it didn't just destroy the mill," Ridge said.

Malachi lowered his hands, and the blue barrier vanished. The debris littering the space between them and the mill testified to how much Malachi's shield had protected them.

Kane and Malachi picked their way through the wreckage while Ridge stood guard in case their indiscretion had attracted attention.

"Looks like the millstones did the job," Malachi reported as he headed for the items in his saddlebag and returned to where Kane was waiting. While the witch added the ingredients called for by the nullification spell, Kane rearranged the splintered wood so that the fire would burn hottest over the cracked and broken stones.

"Henri's going to be sorry he missed this," Ridge remarked as the flames rose, helped by a flicker of Malachi's magic. The fire's glow lit their way as they turned their back on the old mill.

"Don't encourage him," Kane said. "He has a gift for destruction."

"Very true. Probably why he's always been such a good fit with Rett and me," Ridge replied, chuckling despite the situation as they headed back to Rune Keep.

CHAPTER ELEVEN

"What if it doesn't work?" Rett worried aloud as Malachi prepared the ritual elements for the spell.

"Which part?" Malachi chalked symbols on the large piece of slate covering the table and set out candles at the four quarters of the ritual circle. "Getting to Green Knoll, finding Runcian's original spell, fighting off the Witch Lord's attack, or keeping the cloister and its hidden location from vanishing into thin air?"

"All of it. Any of it. The whole thing is dicey," Rett replied.

Malachi reinforced the protective wardings around the doors and windows and made sure the circle on the floor around their workspace was unbroken before carefully stepping back inside.

"Very dicey indeed," Malachi agreed. "And if it doesn't work? We'll figure it out. After all, we have the cloister's entire occult library to research other possibilities, and we might find out how much Brother Kendrick and the others know about magic."

Rett felt less than reassured. Ridge, Henri, and Kane had left a candlemark ago to meet with Gil and Luc to hand over the blackmail box. He wasn't sure which made him more nervous—their rendezvous or the spell and ritual Malachi prepared.

"I've figured out how to do some things better than the last time," Malachi told him and slid a cup of strange smelling liquid toward Rett while keeping one for himself. "This potion will make it easier for us to trance together and remain linked. You may find that it reduces anxiety and also lets you access your abilities more easily."

He lit a bowl of incense, filling the air with its spicy scent. "This will enhance psychic abilities and help you focus," he told Rett.

Since Rett still wasn't entirely clear on what his abilities entailed, he didn't know if loosening his grip on them was a good idea, but he trusted Malachi's experience. Rett pinched his nose shut and swallowed the drink in one gulp, then grimaced and fought the urge to spit.

"Gods, that's awful! Tastes like swamp water!"

Malachi barely managed to hide a similar reaction and looked at the empty glass with distaste. "It's terrible, but it should do the job." They sat facing each other and reached across the table to take hands.

"Take us to Green Knoll, Rett. You lead, and I'll follow."

Rett closed his eyes and focused. He breathed in the candle smoke, tasted the dregs of the foul potion on his tongue, felt Malachi's warm hands gripping his own like an anchor.

As Malachi had taught him, Rett concentrated on his breath and his heartbeat. The leaves and powders in the bowl sent an earthy aroma into the air that made him feel lightheaded. Rett pictured the cloister, visualizing it in detail, making the image as specific as he could until he felt a *shift*.

When he opened his eyes, he and Malachi were in Green Knoll.

They appeared in the dining room, greeted by gasps and the clang and clatter of dropped utensils. Before anyone could grab a knife and attack, Tom ran to stand in front of them, arms flung wide, making himself a protective barrier.

"They're friends," Tom told the others, with a pleading glance toward Kendrick, who stood and nodded.

"Everyone remain calm," Kendrick ordered.

Rett wasn't sure that Kendrick trusted them as much as Tom did, but he was relieved at the response. He looked around the dining room and realized that furniture had been moved to allow sleeping mats to line the floor, and one of the tables had been converted to a research area covered with books, parchment, inkwells, and quill pens. Salt and aconite had been sprinkled across the windowsills and by the entrances, and protective sigils were marked on the glass and the doors.

What's happened? It's as if they're afraid to be out of sight of one another.

"We should talk." Kendrick jerked his head toward the far corner of the room and gestured for them to follow. Rett shot a worried glance at Tom, who just shook his head.

The other monks went back to their tasks, and a quiet hum of conversation resumed. When they reached the corner, Kendrick looked Malachi up and down. "Who are you?"

"A witch. My name is Malachi. We have some ideas on how to help."

"Brother Kendrick found the books that Runcian left about the spell," Tom blurted.

"Runcian told me that he would leave the key to the magic where we could find it in an emergency," Kendrick said. "Then he said that I would only remember when the need was great. I guess that's true because I had a vivid dream about him telling me where to go in the library and how to release the protections on the books. Everything from my dream was true."

"We've been studying the books," Tom added. "But I don't know if we can figure things out fast enough. It's gotten bad."

"Tell us," Rett urged. He could see the worry and strain in both men's faces and knew that something new must have gone wrong since he visited.

"We've had more bad storms and tremors," Kendrick said, clearly uneasy. "Everyone's had nightmares, visions of Green Knoll ceasing to exist. Then yesterday, the land outside the stone fence *wobbled* like ripples in a pool. If I hadn't seen it myself, I wouldn't have believed."

"What do the other monks make of it?" Malachi asked.

"They sense the damage to the energy around us. We're all frightened. From what Rett told us, it's not safe to return to Landria, but we've never had to defend ourselves against an attack here. Just being at Green Knoll was our defense," Kendrick replied.

"I've memorized what we learned from the old books, and I've got the beginning of a ritual that I think will work," Malachi said. "If we put that together with Runcian's notes, we should be able to strengthen the wardings."

"How will that help if someone is attacking from outside?" Tom sounded scared.

Malachi smiled reassuringly. "We have friends targeting the witches who are causing the problem. With us working from inside and our friends on the outside, we stand a good chance of fixing the problem—and stopping the danger from happening again."

Kendrick dragged a hand over his face, and Rett wondered how long the man had gone without sleep. "Let's get to it. Time is running out."

A kettle boiled on the fire in the kitchen, supplying tea and coffee to help keep them awake and a different mixture to ease headaches and sore muscles. Malachi and Kendrick leaned shoulder to shoulder over the old tomes, while Tom and Rett helped by fetching other books, bringing fresh inkwells, and swapping out manuscripts.

It occurred to Rett that the young man next to him was the rightful next king of Landria. Tom might have received an education suitable for a prince, thanks to the foresight of the monks, but at least for now, he had nothing of the posturing which came with the crown. Tom seemed every bit the sheltered monk, close to Rett's age but far less jaded and world-weary.

As relieved as Rett felt about securing a king for Landria that wouldn't be Makary's puppet, he did not envy Tom—Toland—the burdens of the crown.

Outside, the wind howled and rain pelted the shutters. Hail hitting the roof sounded like gunfire. The flames in the fireplace danced wildly as the wind across the chimney drew them upward.

The ground beneath Rett's feet shook, making his coffee slosh and widening a spider web of cracks in the plaster on the walls. Tom looked up, panicked, and met Rett's gaze.

"Keep working," Rett advised quietly. "It's our best shot."

Kendrick paused to walk among the monks, talking with them and trying to calm their fears. Rett looked around and frowned. "Where are the rest?"

"We've taken turns staying in the stables and barn with the animals, always in groups of three," Tom told him. "The quakes frighten the horses, and we don't want them to hurt themselves. All the chores that can be done inside—mending clothing or tack, repairing books, and the like—have been moved so we can remain together. Being with each other might not change the outcome, but it gives us comfort while we await our fate."

Rett reached out and gave Tom's shoulder a reassuring squeeze. "We're going to do everything we can to protect you."

Tom managed an uncertain smile. "I know. We're counting on you."

Malachi beckoned Rett to him, and he obliged with a murmured apology to Tom for leaving him.

"Have you found him? Makary?" Rett asked, anxious for them to begin the working.

"Makary wasn't actually far away," Malachi replied. "He's been stealing energy from Noxx and from the people Noxx made into *kolvry*. That let him hide and also made it possible for him to send the assassin to Green Knoll. But now he can't sustain what he's doing by himself—not and fight us." Malachi gave a wolfish smile. "We can stop him."

"What about Noxx?" Rett feared for Ridge and his friends.

"Makary and Noxx share a bond. The harder we strike at Makary, the more he'll pull energy from Noxx. We might not be able to destroy them, but perhaps we can weaken them past the point where they pose a danger."

"How can I help?" Rett asked.

"It isn't fair for me to ask this of you, but I don't see another way," Malachi replied with a guilty expression.

"Anything I can do, just tell me."

"Kendrick and I believe we've worked out a spell to renew Runcian's original magic and strengthen it against the attacks," Malachi told him. "But we need to know what's going on with Sofen and the witches at Harrowmont—and if they've been able to carry out their part of the plan. I'd like to have you scry so we can coordinate the timing and make their attack count."

The insanity of their plan, such as it was, had not escaped Rett from the beginning. Malachi and Kendrick would use Runcian's spells to strengthen the protection on Green Knoll.

At the same time, Sofen, Gil, and any ghostly helpers they could recruit would launch a psychic attack on Makary and Noxx.

Malachi felt certain that Makary would have to drop whatever magic had been hiding him to work spells powerful enough to disrupt the protections on Green Knoll. Noxx was also likely to reveal himself by using such strong magic. When the Witch Lord and Noxx became findable, Gil and the others would strike—betting that Makary and Noxx couldn't sustain their assault on Green Knoll and defend themselves at the same time.

"I'll do it," Rett said, although his heartbeat quickened in fear at the prospect. "How will it work?"

Tom brought a low, shallow bowl of water to a table near where Malachi and Kendrick would cast their spell.

"The potion we drank and the incense should enable you to scry and see what's happening at Harrowmont. I'll do the scrying spell—but I need you to watch the images. I can't take my attention away from the magic to fight Makary and Noxx."

"Of course. Just tell me what to do."

"Since you're not physically present here in Green Knoll, the scrying will work a little differently," Malachi explained. "More of 'redirecting' your focus, so you're seeing Harrowmont through the image on the water in the bowl. Sofen is watching for you. He'll make the connection with Gil and the ghosts if that's necessary."

Rett stared into the depths of the water as the still surface rippled, and then he saw Harrowmont and Sofen—the young seer whose exceptionally strong psychic gifts made him a prize to be fought over before he had found sanctuary with Lady Sally Anne. The boy had grown since Rett's last visit, but his wide, preternaturally knowing eyes had not changed.

"I see Sofen and the parlor at Harrowmont," Rett reported. "I think he knows that I'm watching. He looked right at me."

"What else did you see?" Malachi asked while Kendrick took up the quiet incantation.

"Sofen and Lorella and a number of others are gathered in the parlor. I'm guessing it's all the psychics and mediums. They were sitting in groups, and no one was talking."

Malachi nodded. "Good. Sofen will find a way to communicate with you if there's something we need to know. Lorella is keeping an eye on Gil and Ridge through the ghosts."

Rett watched the image in the scrying bowl of the group in the far-away parlor. Lorella was there, along with several of the other psychic children Rett recognized. Lady Sally Anne stood in the far corner, a concerned observer.

Someone poured a line of protective salt mixture across the doorway, completing a circle around the walls. Sigils painted on the windows and relics on the parlor bookshelves hadn't been displayed on his previous visits. The haze of incense hung heavy in the air. Though the room was quiet, Rett picked up on tension that reminded him of the eve of battle.

I've been a sniper. I know how it feels to stay separate to get the shot and wait for the right moment to avoid ruining the mission. This is just a different kind of sniper shot, magic instead of matchlock, Rett thought.

"Ready?" Sofen asked the others gathered around him, although when he spoke, he stared right at Rett as if he could see him. *"It's time."*

The ground at the cloister shook beneath their feet, pulling Rett's focus back to Green Knoll.

"We're turning Makary's spell back on him ... he's resisting ... drawing energy from somewhere," Malachi murmured, and Rett wondered if the "window" of the scrying bowl worked both directions, somehow enabling Sofen to know what was going on at Green Knoll.

Rett felt the magic surge both at Green Knoll and Harrowmont. The power crested again, and Rett felt it like whiplash as he bounced from one end of his psychic tether to the other.

He cried out as a wave of fear washed over him, and he fought to breathe. Green Knoll shook to its foundations. Plaster cracked, windows shattered, and shutters banged in the wild storm. Lightning boomed, sending a second shockwave through the cloister.

This felt like Makary's master stroke, the culmination of his attack. The entire chapter house trembled, and the monks cried out—terrified—although they did not leave their places or stop chanting.

Malachi and Kendrick kept up their incantation, working Runcian's spell and reinforcing the protections, even as they ignored the storm that raged outside.

Rett's awareness snapped back to Harrowmont. He could see the psychics sitting in groups of three, holding hands, heads bowed, each group silent until someone gave a cry of triumph or frustration.

Abruptly, the assault on Green Knoll stopped. Rett saw the monks' fear in their faces that this reprieve might be a trick, their worry that Makary was pausing before launching a final, deadly barrage. As the moments without a new attack stretched on, concern shifted to hope.

"It's working … don't stop … don't let him strike again … " Rett conveyed what he heard from Sofen through the scrying. He felt the toll the connection was taking on his mind and body, stretching him gossamer thin as power and magic flowed through his consciousness like fire.

An image flooded Rett's mind of Ridge, Luc, Henri, Gil, and Kane under attack, outnumbered by a horde of Noxx's *kolvry* fighters. Magic had blown Rett's Sight wide open, and the stain that Noxx's tainted magic forced onto the *kolvry* looked like streaks of black ichor.

Malachi's shout jerked Rett's awareness back to Green Knoll. Magic filled the room, so strong Rett thought he might choke on it. A tide of power rose from Malachi and the monks, and Rett feared they were making their last stand. The energy strengthened the wardings surrounding the hidden cloister, and this time, it met Makary's onslaught before the dark mage could breach the perimeter.

The opposing magics warred like well-matched duelists. Makary's magic surged as if he had tapped a hidden reserve, flaring stronger than before. Rett held his breath as Malachi and the monks held steady, even as the rippling power from the psychics at Harrowmont blasted against the Witch Lord's barrage.

Abruptly, the attack on Green Knoll stopped, leaving Rett feeling like he had been leaning into a suddenly becalmed headwind.

Elation carried loud and clear through the bond from Harrowmont as the monks around him at Green Knoll cheered, but unless Gil sent a message to Sofen via their psychic connection, Rett had no way to know the fate of Ridge and the others.

Are they alive? If Makary failed, did Noxx withdraw his kolvry *fighters? Or did we win one battle only to lose another?*

Silence answered his attempts, and after that, darkness.

CHAPTER TWELVE

"Can I go on record saying that I don't like this at all?" Ridge grumbled as he rode with Kane and Henri toward the rendezvous with Gil and Luc. The blackmail box was now tucked safely into Kane's saddlebag. Once Luc took the information back to Kristoph loyalists, the threat posed by a traitorous regency council might be over for good.

"Doesn't make a damn bit of difference," Kane replied. "It's still our best shot at saving the heir—and maybe stop Makary and Noxx."

"If we had Rett with us, Edvard could scout ahead and let us know if Luc was on his way," Ridge continued, in no mood to be placated. "What if Gil and Luc don't show?"

"Then we've ridden a long way for nothing," Kane replied, as sanguine as ever.

A few miles from the meeting place, Henri veered off on a side road with the matchlock to get into position on the hill above the rendezvous spot. Kane had scouted the area in advance so they could lay their plans. Henri was insurance—in case more than magic went wrong.

Ridge knew that his foul mood came from fearing for Rett's safety rather than any doubt that Luc and Gil would arrive. Although he trusted Malachi, Ridge feared that Rett would once again push past his limits, heedless of the cost to himself.

Surviving a battle was never guaranteed. He and Rett had buried too many comrades and barely escaped too many times to take anything for granted. Still, this fight against Makary and Noxx felt so unfairly skewed that Ridge couldn't entirely squash his resentment.

Ridge usually restrained his Sight, afraid of discovery. But without Rett or Malachi, he was the only one of their group to have even a glimmer of extra ability until Gil arrived, and since both Noxx and Makary were in the wind, Ridge feared they would need every advantage.

None of the travelers they had passed so far bore the stain of having sworn themselves to a dark mage. But Ridge knew that a witch could bind people against their will to do his bidding, and that type of magic would elude Ridge's Sight.

Rett will have Malachi summon me and bind my ghost if I'm dumb enough to get myself killed. I made him promise to survive—I'd better do the same.

Nothing about their parallel missions could be considered a "plan" by military standards. They were desperate to pin their hopes on such a scheme.

One step up from wishful thinking is more like it.

Meeting Gil and Luc at a crossroads was as much about drawing out Noxx as it was handing off the information.

I hate being bait.

As they approached the meeting point, Luc rode out from behind a line of trees. "Good to see you're well," he said, giving them an appraising glance.

"Same with you," Ridge replied.

Kane withdrew the wooden box. "There's more than enough information here to disqualify Makary's top candidates for the regency council." Kane handed over the blackmail documents. "Might even land a few of them in irons." He gave a cold smile. "At least we hope so."

Luc slipped the box into his saddlebags and latched the clasp.

"Thanks for meeting us. Gil decided to tag along since you've managed to annoy not one but two evil witches," Luc said.

"Just figured it was as good a time as any to have a medium on hand," Gil replied.

A shot rang out, and hoof beats pounded toward them from both directions.

Ridge and his companions reined in their horses and drew their swords. He glanced down at himself and then at the others, checking for blood, but none of them had been the target of the shot. Gil moved back a few paces, and from the look of contemplation on his face, Ridge bet the medium was reaching out to any spirits within range.

"Over there!" Kane pointed to a slight rise on the other side of the road, where a body sprawled that had not been there moments ago. Ridge guessed Henri had picked off an enemy sniper.

"Henri, you're a damn fine shot," Ridge murmured.

Six men dressed in the uniform of King's Shadows closed in on them, three from each side, swords in hand. Clearly, they didn't come to talk.

A blond man urged his horse forward a few steps and held up a piece of parchment. He regarded them with an expression of withering disgust and condescension.

"You are all under arrest as traitors to the crown, complicit in the murder of King Kristoph. This writ of execution empowers me to—"

"Kill us. We know. I used to be in the same business if you remember," Ridge snapped. He recognized the men's faces, although he couldn't put names to them. All of them were Shadows who had despised him and Rett.

A second shot sent a flock of nearby birds flying as the matchlock bullet tore through the leader's shoulder, taking him off his saddle and landing him on his ass in the dirt.

Henri had time to reload. Good shot!

"You just shot a King's Shadow!" one of the other newcomers yelped in protest.

"Good thing you won't be around to report us, now isn't it?" Ridge urged his horse to charge in case any of them decided to go after Henri. He rode at the assassins at full speed. Luc and Kane veered apart to attack from the sides while the downed man scrambled to avoid being trampled. Gil stayed where he was, but the temperature plummeted, and Ridge guessed the ghosts had heeded Gil's call.

Ridge blocked a sword thrust meant to kill and in response delivered a deep gash across his attacker's ribs with the long knife in his left hand. He ducked and pivoted as his second adversary swung at him, unable to dodge the blow completely. The blade sliced his left bicep, sending warm blood running down his arm.

Kane and Luc fought their targets, drawing them away from Ridge. Neither of Ridge's attackers gave ground despite their wounds, and while he held them off, he knew he couldn't keep them at bay for long.

They were outnumbered, but Ridge had seen far worse odds. Ridge tried to avoid killing the Shadows, although he wasn't above a maiming blow that might change their choice of vocation.

A third shot tumbled one of the attackers from his mount. Ridge couldn't see whether the man was dead. Their pursuers had made a big error in overlooking Henri.

Ridge parried, and the force of the strike reverberated down his arm. Their blades locked, and he slid their swords together, closing the gap as his knife dug into the assassin's ribs.

"Surrender, and I'll let you live," Ridge growled.

"Not when I can claim the bounty." The attacker twisted and threw off Ridge's sword then slashed his knife across Ridge's thigh.

Ridge bit back a cry of pain. His opponent seized the advantage, coming at him with a flurry of strikes. Blood ran down his leg and into his boot. Ridge fought to stay in the saddle as numbness warred with pain. *I might lose this fight. Rett will never forgive me.*

Out of his peripheral vision, Ridge saw that Luc and Kane still fought their assassins.

Henri fired, but his shot went wide, frightening one of the horses. Kane took advantage of his opponent's momentary distraction to disarm the man and shove him from his mount.

More hoof beats thundered closer, and Ridge doubted that he and his friends could fight their way clear of reinforcements. Another shot sounded, close at hand, and friend and foe alike stared at the newcomers.

Burke held his matchlock pointed at the sky. Caralin's rifle aimed at the head of Ridge's opponent. Four rogue Shadows accompanied them.

"Relieve the brigands of their weapons and restrain them," Burke ordered.

Ridge and Kane exchanged a glance, unsure who Burke meant. When the rogue Shadows went straight for the traitors,

Ridge breathed a quiet sigh of relief. *That could have gone the other way.*

"Sheriff," Burke said with a glance at Luc, who nodded in acknowledgment. Then he looked to Ridge. "Call your valet down from the high ground. He's got an itchy trigger finger."

Kane slipped down from his saddle and grabbed a rolled bandage from his saddlebag. "After I bind up Ridge's leg, we'll answer your questions."

"How did you know where to find us?" Ridge ignored Burke's request for the moment. He shifted, giving Kane access to wrap his wound tightly, staunching the flow of blood although it still hurt like a son of a bitch.

"Hard to ignore when a ghost ices over a window and writes a note," Burke replied in a dry tone. His team hustled the bound and injured attackers over to the side of the road and gathered their horses while Caralin kept her rifle trained on the prisoners.

Ridge guessed that Gil had found a ghostly messenger. Burke and the others ignored Gil, and Ridge wondered whether they knew who he was and deferred to his rank or if a deflection charm made them overlook the medium.

Henri fired again, aiming at a spot down the eastern road. Ridge, Burke, and the others turned in shock as dozens of battered, bleeding, and bleary-eyed *kolvry* ambled toward them.

"Shit." Ridge glanced at Burke and Caralin. "Got any more of those matchlocks?"

Caralin shook her head. "No. But we can go to the high ground with Henri. He's not going to shoot us, is he?"

"Of course not," Ridge replied. "Probably," he added quietly, earning a scowl from Burke.

Burke turned to his team. "I can't believe I'm saying this." He raised his voice. "Breckinridge is in charge. Fight about it later." With that, he rode up the hill behind Caralin.

The glowers that greeted Ridge made it clear all was not for-given. "Guard the prisoners," Ridge said to one of the ex-Shadows. "Everyone else, block the road. Make the monsters come to us. Let the snipers do their job and don't get in their way."

"That's it? Stand here and wait to be attacked?" One of Burke's men spat.

Ridge sensed the shifting chill and guessed that the front line of ghosts put themselves between the living and the *kolvry*, providing a first line of defense.

The tug of magic made Ridge look up to a hill well out of firing range on the other side of the road where he saw a man silhouetted against the sky.

Noxx. Don't know how he found out where we'd be, but I'm glad he took the bait. Now here's hoping Gil and Sofen keep their part of the deal.

"Hold steady," Ridge called out. "And no matter what—keep your position."

"What do you think we're going to see, Breckenridge? Faeries?" The ex-Shadow beside Ridge sneered.

"No," Ridge replied in a calm voice as the first of the *kolvry* met Gil's reinforcements. "Ghosts—and magic."

Poisons and torture had broken the minds and spirits of the twisted foot soldiers Noxx sent against them, and cruel magic had drained their souls while vengeful ghosts possessed their bodies. Their danger lay in numbers and in their unrea-soning rage, making them eager to tear apart anything that got in their way.

"What ... is ... that?" The cocky assassin who had mocked Ridge moments before paled as invisible adversaries wrestled the *kolvry* to the ground, clawing at their skin and leaving marks from phantom blows.

"Ghosts," Ridge replied with a grin, knowing Gil had sent out a call for backup. "Allies. We'll deal with the ones who get past them—if any do."

The ex-Shadows' training held true, and they held their positions. From the rise behind them, Henri, Burke, and Caralin fired into the *kolvry* horde, staggering the shots and reloads for a near-constant barrage. Nothing slowed the creatures, and Ridge wondered if they retained enough of their former selves to welcome oblivion.

Safe for the moment, Ridge turned his attention back to Noxx, who still stood with his arms lifted high, orchestrating the advance of his twisted army. *Come on, Gil. Anytime now would be great for you to take Noxx out of the game.*

In the next breath, Ridge saw Noxx stagger. On the road in front of Ridge, the *kolvry* faltered, hesitating and losing their way as the spirits doubled their attack.

One of the *kolvry* stumbled out of the roadway, almost skirting the ghostly blockade, only to die on the edge of a Shadow's blade. Ridge could tell that the flagrant magic and the obvious ability to coordinate a ghostly attack had badly rattled the assassins.

Movement on the far hilltop pulled Ridge from his thoughts. Noxx still stood, although his movements were jerky and uncoordinated as if he was trying to grab hold of something he couldn't see.

Suddenly Noxx's head fell back. Flames engulfed his body, and he burned bright as a beacon until his charred form fell to the ground in a dark heap.

"What in the name of the Abyss was that?" The man behind Ridge yelped.

"That was Makary's witch, catching fire," Ridge replied, ignoring the gaping mouths and horrified stares of his companions.

"What's happening?" One of the former assassins pointed, and the others turned.

The *kolvry* stood frozen without someone to control them as the ghosts choked them and tore limbs from bodies. Some of the *kolvry* sank to the ground, twitching and groaning, bloodshot eyes pleading silently for the release of death.

"The ghosts possessing the *kolvry* have no agenda without their master. The people won't survive having the ghosts pulled out of them. All we can do is give them a quick death," Ridge ordered. "They can't be saved. It's a mercy."

The ex-Shadows cursed under their breath, making no secret of their revulsion, but they followed orders, wading in among the dying creatures to deliver killing blows. They shivered as they moved among the ghosts they couldn't see, spirits that didn't bother to get out of their way.

Ridge turned to Gil. "Is Noxx really dead?"

Gil didn't open his eyes, still communicating with the ghosts he summoned, but he gave a curt nod.

"Thank you," Ridge said quietly.

"You're a witch now, Breckenridge?" The former assassin next to Ridge rounded on him. Ridge couldn't remember the man's name.

"No. I just see the soul stain of the disloyal. Get over it—or I might look a little too closely at *your* soul," Ridge threatened, eyes narrowed.

Seeing the assassin's eyes go wide and having him take a half step back made Ridge's lips quirk in a half-smile.

"That's … ah … a handy asset in a battle," the man said, practically stumbling over himself not to offend the "witch."

"It certainly is." Ridge fixed him with a look and wondered if his unwilling companion would spend the rest of the day worried about sprouting warts and hungering for flies.

Burke, Caralin, and Henri descended from the rise with their matchlocks over their shoulders. They took in the bloody bodies sprawled across the roadway, and from Henri's expression Ridge knew their valet could figure out the meaning of the chill in the air.

"Is it over?" Henri asked.

Ridge nodded toward the hill where Noxx's charred remains lay. "I think so. At least our piece of it."

He sighed. "It won't bring Kristoph back. But his killers are dead, and we've stopped yet another of Makary's schemes to seize the crown."

Burke regarded Ridge with a frown. "Where's Rett?"

"If we're lucky, he's saving a place that doesn't exist," Ridge replied. Given the uncertain loyalties of the former Shadows—aside from Burke and Caralin—he had no desire to put Tom or Green Knoll in further danger.

Caralin's eyes narrowed. "I told you he wouldn't give you a straight answer."

Burke met Ridge's gaze and held it for a moment, making Ridge wonder just how much the Shadow Master knew. "Oh, I think he did. In his own way." He turned to survey the mess. "Very well. Ridge, take your people and leave before I change my mind."

Burke looked at the former Shadows. "Guess we'll have to figure out what to do with the bodies—and the traitors who survived," he said with a sigh. "Too bad the ghosts didn't get them."

"That can be arranged." Ridge couldn't help himself.

Burke gave him a steely glare. "Go. Do not test my forbearance."

Caralin snorted since everyone knew that Ridge's very existence stretched Burke's patience. "Good luck with that," she murmured.

"What did you say?" Burke growled.

"Nothing," she said, clearing her throat. "Nothing important."

Ridge, Kane, Henri, Gil, and Luc rode away while the others quibbled. Luc and Gil took their leave at the first crossroads.

"I'll get this to the right people in the palace—Kristoph's loyalists who don't want the Witch Lord's puppets on the Regency Council," Gil promised. "Thank you for finding the information we need to stop them."

"Don't forget that Burke is sheltering witnesses who can connect prominent people directly to Kristoph's murder," Ridge reminded him. "Together with what's in that box, you should have everything you need. Makary's supporters will be lucky not to end up clapped in irons." He paused. "Can you tell how Rett and Malachi are doing at Green Knoll?"

Gil closed his eyes, concentrating. "They're alive, and they've been fighting off Makary, making him pull energy from Noxx. That made a big difference in our fight—and it's why Noxx went up in flames."

With a jaunty salute, Luc and Gil rode toward the city while Ridge and the others turned the other direction.

"You're bleeding through the bandage," Henri said. "We need to stop and bind that up again. You're pale as a ghost."

Ridge didn't protest when Henri made them pause beside a stream. Kane kept watch while Henri soaked a rag in water and cleaned the gash, covering it with a poultice and binding it with fresh strips of linen to prevent infection and stop the blood loss.

"You're lucky you didn't lose more blood," Henri chided. "Or you'd be slung face-down across your saddle like a dead deer."

"I'm grateful for small favors."

Henri made a rude noise. "That's all right—I'm sure Rett will want my full report."

"We can make a deal."

Henri raised an eyebrow. "Oh?"

"We need to keep moving unless you want to die," Kane warned. "Noxx wasn't the only danger."

I'm trusting Rett to survive and keep up his side of the bargain so he can tell me the rest of the story. He'd better be there, in one piece, when I get back, Ridge thought.

Chapter Thirteen

"How long have I been out?" Rett asked when he woke with a dry mouth and a scratchy throat. Ridge sat in a chair near his bed, disheveled and exhausted, with a new growth of beard that gave Rett some idea about the answer.

"Too long." Ridge leaned forward to help Rett sit up and then held a glass of water for him to drink. "Days. Malachi had to compel you to eat and drink, but you didn't really wake up for any of it."

Rett noticed that Ridge's right leg was propped on a footstool and raised an eyebrow.

"Got slashed on the leg and arm. Long story. I'll tell you later. I'm healing, but it still hurts. I'll have a limp for a while, and it'll take time to strengthen my arm," Ridge said with a sheepish smile.

"You all came back safe?" Rett took a few more sips of water and then sank back onto the mattress.

"Yeah," Ridge answered. "It could have been a lot worse. Fortunately, Henri's a good shot, Gil and his ghost friends are bad-asses, and Burke showed up with reinforcements. That let us hold off the 'new' Shadows loyal to the Witch Lord and Noxx's *kolvry*. Gil said you and Malachi made Makary draw from Noxx's energy enough to kill him. Thanks for that, by the way." He paused. "What about Green Knoll?"

"Malachi and the monks reinforced Runcian's spell and kicked Makary's assassin out on his ass," Rett told him. "Sofen and Lorella and the others with abilities at Harrowmont helped to harass Noxx and Makary and provoke them to overextend themselves."

"Did Malachi bring Brother Tom and the others back with him?"

Rett shook his head. "They didn't find out how to reverse the spell, just how to strengthen the original magic. Malachi's studying it, but he doesn't have an answer yet. And honestly, until we can end Makary, Green Knoll is the safest place for Tom."

"Harrowmont?"

"Edvard checked in with Lorella and Sofen. Everyone is safe, and the siege is over. They sent Duke Foster's soldiers running with their tails between their legs. Turns out he was mentioned in those blackmail documents. Seems he was implicated in helping to plan Kristoph's murder," Ridge said. "I think his besieging days are over. He'll be lucky to avoid the gallows."

Rett knew he wasn't completely recovered, but he'd been bedridden long enough. He felt stiff and sore, and he smelled sweat-sour even to himself. "I need to get clean," he told Ridge. "If you can bring me a basin of water, a towel, and clothes, I'll take care of it." He managed a tired smile. "Thanks for putting up with my stink."

"If it means you came home alive, I'm willing to let you stink up the place all you want." Ridge sighed. "You had us all scared again. I'm grateful for what you did. Maybe there wasn't another option, but dammit—I'd like for us all to live through saving the kingdom."

"We might not."

Ridge looked away and nodded. "I know that. But we've made it this far. If we can kill Makary and put Tom—Toland—on the throne, then as far as I'm concerned, our work is done. We've got money put aside. Henri could find us all a nice place at the seaside. We could open a pub and only have to worry about bad-tempered drunks."

Rett had to admit that Ridge's daydream held a lot of appeal. "Stop being Shadows?"

"I wouldn't want to work for anyone but Burke, and I imagine the new king will want his own people," Ridge replied. "The other Shadows would still rather feed us to the pigs than collaborate. So—fuck them. We've been at this for almost a decade, longer than most assassins last. Once we save the kingdom, I think we've earned our freedom."

Rett smiled. "I like that idea." He sighed. "But we're not done yet."

"You're right—unfortunately. But we're closer than before. So hang onto the idea about the pub, and maybe that'll pull us through." Ridge stood. "I'll go get water for you. Malachi and Henri have supper cooking. Kane will be back later—he went to meet with Luc. I imagine he'll have news when he returns."

Rett took his time getting clean, enjoying the warm water and the smell of soap. He did the best he could with his hair and resigned himself to cutting it shorter. Clean clothing and fresh sheets felt like the height of luxury, and he felt grateful all over again for Malachi's help and his willingness to offer them sanctuary. By the time he ventured into the main room, Rett felt presentable.

"Good to see you up and about," Henri greeted him. "Eat hearty—you need to put some meat back on your bones." He bustled to the fireplace to fix Rett a bowl of stew and carried it to the table, where Malachi and Ridge were already seated.

Malachi studied Rett in silence for a moment, probably using his magic to ascertain how well the healing had progressed. Finally, he nodded. "Your energy is definitely better. And since I didn't get to tell you before you passed out—nice work."

Rett hoped no one expected conversation because his stomach rumbled, and he dug into his food like a starving man. Kane joined them mid-meal and promised an update after he made quick work of his meal.

Later, Malachi brought out a jug of whiskey and a plate of Henri's fruit tarts. They lingered at the table, not settled enough to play cards but delaying yet another serious conversation as long as possible.

Finally, Kane broke the silence. "Gil passed the blackmail information to one of Kristoph's loyal advisors. The arrests have already begun. Burke turned the witnesses over to Luc, who smuggled them into the city. They're safely hidden at Gil's family's estate until the loyalists in the palace can bring the traitors up on charges. It won't bring Kristoph back, but it does clean some of the rats out of the palace."

"Have you found Kristoph's spirit?" Rett asked, glancing at Malachi.

The necromancer shook his head. "No. I've been a bit busy keeping you from becoming a ghost. But from some of the manuscripts I had a chance to read at Green Knoll, I think I know why Makary trapped Kristoph's spirit."

He took a sip of his drink. "The ghosts of the past kings play a part in the coronation ceremony. There's an invocation that conveys protection and unlocks some special ability—not sure what—for the legitimate monarch. Maybe an ancestral chain of memory that gets updated by the ghosts?" Malachi shrugged. "Kendrick is going to keep looking for details. We'll need to know what's required to make sure Tom fulfills all the ceremonial requirements."

"And Runcian?" Rett felt like he had a lot of catching up to do. "Did you find his spirit?"

Malachi shook his head. "No. I can't prove it, but I think Runcian died working the original spell to hide and protect Green Knoll. He knew what was at stake. Death magic is usually forbidden, but it can be extremely powerful. He may have given his life to protect the heir and his soul was forced to move on."

Rett felt the whiskey warm him and he savored the taste. "So much has happened, but the Witch Lord always manages to get away."

"Not forever," Ridge said, with a finality in his voice that told Rett his partner wouldn't rest until Makary had paid for his treachery. "We've harrowed his followers, spoiled his plans, and forced him into hiding. Once the trials begin for the regency council candidates, Makary's supporters are likely to distance themselves to save their own necks. And he's lost his mage—Noxx is dead."

Kane leaned forward. "Speaking of which—how did Noxx go up in flames?"

Rett's eyebrows rose in surprise. "He what?"

"I saw it happen," Ridge said. "One minute he was controlling his *kolvry* fighters, and the next, he went up like a torch."

Rett searched his memories since he had been scrying Harrowmont at the time. "I have to admit, by the time we got that far I was already stretched thin. I don't remember."

Malachi leaned back in his chair. "You don't remember because Sofen and the others didn't do it. Makary did." He lifted a hand to silence their surprised outbursts. "Kendrick and the monks and I were sending powerful magic against Makary's assault on Green Knoll. Sofen and the psychics attacked Makary once he had to show himself."

He shrugged. "I think Makary's bond to Noxx wasn't broken when the garnet shattered. If he kept drawing from Noxx while Noxx was using his own power to force the *kolvry* to attack, Noxx couldn't sustain that. It burned him up."

"Damn," Ridge said. "On the other hand, he had it coming. Can't say I'm sorry about it—saved us the bother."

"Being rid of Noxx is good, but Makary will probably find another fool willing to help him for dreams of glory," Kane said.

"We found the heir and kept him safe. Makary's Regency Council scheme fell apart. Burke and Caralin are back in the game. And we're all alive," Malachi reminded them. "I think that's pretty damn good, considering."

There had been plenty of moments when Rett had been certain they were all going to die, but somehow they'd made it through. Considering how badly damaged he had been when they rescued him from Letwick, Rett counted himself lucky to be in his right mind and functioning. That he had gained new abilities and learned to—mostly—control them astounded him even as their potential still frightened him.

He looked around the table at his companions. Their circle had grown to include Kane and Malachi and their friends at Harrowmont, as well as Gil and Luc. Rett thought again of Ridge's daydream about running a pub when they were done saving the kingdom. He knew that from now on, while he was fighting for Landria, he would also be fighting for that future, to sit down with the friends who had become their family and raise a pint when the battle was finally over.

Rett lifted his glass of whiskey in a toast. "To the future."

ACKNOWLEDGMENTS

Thank you so much to my editor, Jean Rabe, to my husband and writing partner Larry N. Martin for all his behind-the-scenes hard work, and to my wonderful cover artists, Adrijus Guscia and Natania Barron. Thanks also to the Shadow Alliance street team for their support and encouragement and to my fantastic beta readers Trevor, Andrea, and Laurie and the ever-growing legion of ARC readers. And of course, to my "convention gang" of fellow authors for making road trips fun.

About the Author

Gail Z. Martin writes urban fantasy, epic fantasy, and steampunk for Solaris Books, Orbit Books, Falstaff Books, SOL Publishing, and Darkwind Press. Urban fantasy series include *Deadly Curiosities* and the *Night Vigil* (Sons of Darkness). Epic fantasy series include *Darkhurst, The Chronicles of The Necromancer, The Fallen Kings Cycle, The Ascendant Kingdoms Saga, and The Assassins of Landria*. Under her urban fantasy MM paranormal romance pen name of Morgan Brice, she has five series (*Witchbane, Badlands, Kings of the Mountain, Fox Hollow,* and *Treasure Trail*) with more books and series to come.

Co-authored with Larry N. Martin are *Iron and Blood*, the first novel in the Jake Desmet Adventures series and the *Storm and Fury* collection; and the *Spells, Salt, & Steel*: New Templars series (Mark Wojcik, monster hunter), as well as the *Wasteland Marshals* series and *The Joe Mack Adventures*.

Gail's work has appeared in more than forty US/UK anthologies. Newest anthologies include: *Across the Universe, Release the Virgins, Tales from the Old Black Ambulance, Witches Warriors and Wise Women, Afterpunk: Steampunk Tales of the Afterlife. Christmas at Caynham Castle, Trick or Treat at Caynham Castle, Ring in the New at Caynham Castle, The Four ???? of the Apocalypse, Nevermore, and Three Time Travelers*.

Join the Shadow Alliance street team so you never miss a new release! Get the scoop first + giveaways + fun stuff! Also where Gail and Larry get their beta readers and Launch Team! https://www.facebook.com/groups/435812789942761

Find out more at www.GailZMartin.com, on Twitter @ GailZMartin, at her blog at www.DisquietingVisions.com, on Goodreads https://www.goodreads.com/GailZMartin and on Bookbub https://www.bookbub.com/profile/gail-z-martin. Join the newsletter and get free excerpts at http://eepurl.com/dd5XLj

On Instagram: https://www.instagram.com/morganbrice-author/

On Pinterest: http://www.pinterest.com/gzmartin

Gail is also a con-runner for ConTinual, the online, ongoing multi-genre convention that never ends. www.Facebook.com/Groups/ConTinual

ABOUT THE PUBLISHER

This book is published on behalf of the author by the Ethan
Ellenberg Literary Agency.
https://ethanellenberg.com
Email: agent@ethanellenberg.com
Facebook: https://www.facebook.com/EthanEllenbergLit-
eraryAgency/

Printed in Great Britain
by Amazon

38686948R00136